The BONG-RIPPING BRIDES

COUNT of DROGADO

A NOVEL BY DAVE K

Cover art and interior illustrations by Niki Koch.

Designed by Ian Anderson.

Published and distributed by
Mason Jar Press
Baltimore, MD 21218

Learn more about Mason Jar Press at masonjarpress.xyz.

I am not a human being. This is just a dream,
and soon I will awake.

—Per Yngve Ohlin

PROLOGUE

An old woman stands in what is left of a once-impressive house. Above her, a distended stomach of clouds threatens a storm. Her hands and shirtsleeves are covered in thick black sludge, and she wipes them on her tattered skirt.

As she digs through the rubble, she finds bones scattered throughout the debris, jutting out at odd angles. She finds them under doors, concealed by piles of bricks and lumber, stuffed into cabinets. A pit, dug beneath the house and concealed by a false floor, contains hundreds of intact bodies stacked up like cord wood. They are bloated and discolored, warped by their own weight and the added pressure of time.

Dried blood makes dust that thickens the air and attracts plump, black flies. The old woman swats them away even though she can't touch them, and they can't see her. She separates the bones as best she can, and plucks coins from ash-blackened skulls, knowing by instinct where their ears would have been. These coins are worn and eroded, a few are just flat lumps of carbon. The most deteriorated of these comes from a skeleton whose skull had been crushed at the bottom of a staircase.

Upon concluding this errand, she counts two hundred and eleven coins. This last corpse at her feet will make an even one hundred twelve.

She looks down at it, or what's left of it, and drags it from the rubble to examine it more closely. The face, ribcage, and right arm are all fractured, the left arm has been removed below the shoulder. The cut is relatively clean, and at an angle too precise to blame on an accident. A surgeon's bone saw removed that arm.

The old woman realizes that she has seen this person before. He has seen her, and spoken to her. She remembers him confronting her outside the hovel he shared with those women.

Slowly, with care, she pulls as much of this man as she can find from the wreckage, laying his bones down next to her white bicycle. A bag appears in her right hand, and she lays his bones into it, one by one, before riding away.

THE BONG-RIPPING BRIDES

of COUNT DROGADO

PART I

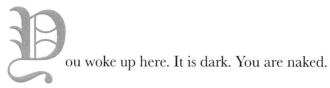ou woke up here. It is dark. You are naked.

There is a bruise under your ribcage. The floor is cool and smooth. You roll onto your stomach before standing. Your knees pop as they straighten. You pass your hand in front of your face and see nothing.

Walking now, each step timid. All you can hear is each foot peeling off the floor, your pulse eddying through your ears, the dry whine of air passing through your nostrils. The air is thick in this room, the smell of smoke potent.

You are a brute in the dark. Your knee bumps against the edge of a table, your shin catches a wooden rack that clatters as it hits the ground. Your foot tangles itself in a shirt, or a large rag. You grab it and toss it away.

You walk now as you walked last night, staggering out of an oyster cellar smelling of rail liquor, melted butter, garlic. Leaning on the iron railing as you lurched up the stairs and into the street, your left jacket sleeve empty and flapping in the breeze.

As you reflect, you clutch and pull at your nakedness. You grope around in the dark, trying to visualize your surroundings. The only clear picture in your head is a red light, pulsing to the waves of dull pain drifting up from your ribs. What feels like an unbound deck of cards slips out from under your hand. You just know those went everywhere.

A crack in the floor brings to mind the topography of your mother's hands, bones bulging under tight skin.

A lantern. You hope there is some oil in it. There is. It emits a soft glow of light the color of chicken fat, and reveals this room to be stocked with amusements. One corner of the room is heaped with athletic equipment that partly obscures a thick red smear on the wall behind it. You find two billiards tables, a range of cues, crates of duck pins and bocce balls and croquet mallets.

Holding the lantern in hand, you investigate the bocce ball set. That's a game for old men, you think to yourself. You try to relate this observation to something about your current circumstances, but nothing comes to you. Some of the bocce balls are spattered red.

You also discover that, yes, you did spill a deck of cards all over the floor. Idiot.

Sometimes you still feel your missing arm, don't you? It's a cruel trick to play upon a man, to take his arm and not his memories of it.

You can hear faint voices and your back stiffens as they get closer and closer. You search with the lantern for a place to hide. The voices sound like singing. Overhead lights flick on and startle you. Your eyes ache and you turn away. You try to hide your shame and drop the lantern.

Those voices are closer now, and more familiar. Did you hear them last night? You try to retrace your steps and ignore the bright lights exposing your nakedness, your stump of a left shoulder.

As you recall, your evening had been soured by a pack of rustics occupying the rear booth seats. Two men. A woman. Four children. You couldn't look at them. Instead, you stared out the window and watched day wilt into evening. You hoped the woman sitting next to you wouldn't ask about your arm and she didn't. There wasn't enough space in her blathering about how she'd *just spent a week with her son up in Coal Country and he's doing well but my everything's so flat there and dirty ugh the air is gray not like the city at all* to ask how you were doing.

You didn't answer much beyond a few token grunts here and there. Was she lonely, do you think? She was an older woman and here was this quiet young man who didn't have any gray in his whiskers yet. You probably reminded her of her son.

After you left, you barged into a conversation on the sidewalk. Demanded cigarettes. You don't even smoke. One of the gentlemen was coarse with you, and you spat in his face, then forced yourself to laugh and not think about the beggarly family trying to build new lives in a world that crushed their old ones. More and more of these rural families pass through the city gates, just as you did. And just like you, they have been left wretched and shabby, their clothes falling into rags. Their gray complexions, guttural speech, the dark consonance of their eyes, these will mark them as targets for every foul intention in the city.

Did you see that steamcoach's headlamps? You were singing *My life is like the summer rose/That opens to the morning sky/But ere the shades of evening close/Is scattered on the ground to die* and rolling down the street like a hat caught in a windstorm.

That man in whose face you spat, was he tall or short? Round build? Well dressed in a dark green suit and eggshell vest. Good, fashionable boots. Spectacles fouled by your hot, beery breath. This man, who could have also been a slender with a mottled complexion and a waxed brown mustache, took his lady companion's arm and hurried across the street.

Who else did you bother? You turned down the wrong alley and almost walked into a man dressed in white. He was ripping his way through a handful of cigarettes, smoking each one down to the end and then using that to light the next one. You guessed that he was a cook. Cooks always smoke like that.

"Watch where you're going!" he said. "Almost dropped these." He clutched his cigarettes in a fist.

"What's the number one cause of divorce?" you asked him. His eyes narrowed, so you repeated yourself.

"I don't know," he said.

"Marriage!" you said. It was a joke you'd overheard in that oyster cellar and, for whatever reason, chosen to share. You laughed much harder than the cook did, of course.

Yes, you saw those headlamps. When it was too late.

Passing by an *al fresco* restaurant, where people ate outdoors at umbrella-shielded tables, your empty jacket sleeve brushed through someone's plate. He was very cross about it. You said something rude to him, which only escalated things. Forks and knives rested on their plates as other people halted their conversations to watch yours as it got louder and uglier.

Now, what did he look like? Was his face well scrubbed with yellow soap? With whom was he eating? A woman? Did you say anything to her? It doesn't matter. You were ordered to leave by the restaurant's waitstaff and you quickened your pace down the street, the man's continued insults rolling down your back.

It was then, as you brushed crumbs and sauce from your useless jacket sleeve, that you noticed a black steamcoach parked in the crosswalk. The engine was idling, and as it lingered while other coaches and pedestrians passed it by, one of its soot-blackened windows rolled down just enough to let a mouthful of smoke blow out into the evening.

You turned away, walking faster. Much like their horse-drawn contemporaries, steamcoaches usually had some manner of ornamentation about them. This coach was sleek and black, with nothing announcing its manufacturer or type. That in and of itself was an announcement. You were right not to trust it.

Maybe if you hadn't looked back, the coach would have lost interest and disappeared down a side street. It could have been the centerpiece for an exaggerated story you told in public houses and saloons, or something neutral to tell yourself.

But you did look back, and the headlamps flicked on. It followed you as you ran from it, light splashing around and in front of you.

You ran with strength you didn't know you had, thundering down sidewalks and across wide cobblestone streets, straying far from your intended path, well outside any familiar bus routes. You hadn't run that fast in a long time.

You cut through a section of burnt-out buildings, hoping
to lose your pursuer in the dark; streetlamps weren't
evenly spaced in that part of the city. The houses
and shops you passed were vacant and crumbling on
top of one another. Fires had turned the area into a
ghetto in mere weeks. It had never been a prosperous
neighborhood, and at its best was like the working classes
who occupied it; quiet and mostly agreeable, if a bit worn
at the edges. Now it was a transient, unwelcoming place.
The normal rhythms of the city were absent. Instead of
coaches and horses and bustle and noise, you heard scraps
of rude language muttered, in accents thick and ugly,
from unlit doorways and alleys.

No matter where you ran, the coach's headlamps
found you.

You ran from the coach until you turned down a side
street and found yourself at a dead end. The coach
negotiated the narrow alley with unexpected grace, its
self-firing front engine exposed to the open air like the
thorax of some giant insect. The sight of it spun you right
off your plate.

"Leave me alone," you said. "I've done nothing to you."
The coach idled for a moment before the lights shut off. You
coughed and backed away until your heel caught the edge of
a rotting wooden pallet and you sagged to the ground.

"What do you want?" you asked the figure that stepped out of the steamcoach. No answer. "I don't have any money," you told him, or her, or it. "Or anything. I don't have anything." The figure was holding something that caught the light. It looked enough like a weapon that you tried scrambling to your feet, intending to run. Then, the sharp pain in your side. You blinked and the world turned sideways. You remember flailing and knocking over a stack of empty crates. Then nothingness.

Then you woke up here, in the dark.

"Hello?" you call out, naked, holding the lantern. "Can anyone hear me? Hello?"

Three women step into the room, singing in alien harmony. *Here comes a candle to light you to bed, here comes a chopper to chop off your head.* They all wear loose white dresses. The woman on the left is wearing white lace gloves, the women in the middle wears a garland of dandelions around her head, and the woman on the right wears her hair unbound, so it hangs in her face.

They are not heavily built, but your father would have called them "good breeding stock." As a farmer, he could never escape that vocabulary.

Chip chop chip chop the last man is dead, they sing, smiling in the sterile light of this room.

The woman wearing lace gloves is carrying a large canvas bag, stained red on the inside. She tosses it in a corner.

The women introduce themselves from left to right as Alice, Beatrice, and Clara.

Alice walks to one of the tall wooden shelves in the room and kneels down. Clara stands on her shoulders and retrieves a blown-glass water pipe from a high shelf.

You knew someone with a similar instrument, back before you lost your arm. He called it a "bong."

Clara's bong is vaguely shaped like a lamp, and solid black, with a squat, round body and a long neck. She steps down onto the floor as Alice slips behind you and pins your arm up behind your back. A spark of pain shoots up your elbow. Her grip is too strong to break.

You watch Clara remove the slide piece and pack the bowl with crumbs of marijuana. Her movements are smooth, practiced, ritualistic. She lights the bowl with a match and inhales slowly. You watch smoke rise up the neck, barely visible behind the black glass.

"What's your name?" she asks you, as you squirm in Alice's grip. The pain in your ribs, the all-consuming unfamiliarity of your situation, and now Clara blowing smoke in your face are too much for your system. You answer her question with a stream of loose vomit that she is just quick enough to avoid.

"I am not apologizing for that," you say, your guts and throat burning.

Clara passes the bong to Beatrice, who takes a hit. "We asked what your name is," Beatrice says. "It's rude not to introduce yourself to a lady who begs an introduction." She passes the bong back to Clara.

"Ma'am, I am naked and have just now thrown up," you say, as Alice's grip loosens. "Both of which are your fault. Not to offend, but your compass for propriety is out of balance."

Clara pulls deeply from the bong and Alice punches you full in the face. Your eyes water and you stagger backwards as pain conflicts with a stupid, chivalrous urge to hide your shameful male body. The back of your head strikes the wall hard enough to clack your teeth together. You wipe blood away from your nose and lip, feeling a weight swing freely between your legs.

"Tell us your name, and you may play a game with us," Clara says, passing the bong back to Beatrice.

"Yes, let's play something," Beatrice says. "We're bored."

You shut your eyes tight.

"Sir." Alice speaks with a voice that could suffocate birds.

"Your name."

You slide down the wall and open your eyes. There is a long red stain on the ceiling, as though something had been dragged across it. "Thomas Carey," you say.

The women break into hearty laughter and coughing fits, and Alice draws deeply from the bong. You pull your knees up to your chest, but your vitals pop out between your thighs. You are reminded of one of your father's dogs, who used to spend entire days in one of the unfinished sheds, cooling himself on the dirt floor.

Beatrice and Alice grab your legs and pull you away from the wall, not letting you shrivel from their gaze, which all but leaves welts on you. Your nose and ribs throb out of sync with each other. They can see the whole of you, which is not whole.

"Hold still," Alice says, exhaling smoke. "We need to dress you." Clara squeals and smiles at what remains of your left arm, cupping the stump in her hands. They push you down even as you flail from side to side, thrashing in their grip. Clara is wearing perfume. You can only get hints of it through the room's heavy smell. She bends over you as Beatrice holds your legs down and Alice pulls an armful of clothes from a hidden closet. The jacket has an officer's cut, with a tapered waist. The trousers and vest are white.

Clara's face is close enough to kiss yours. Her thick, dark hair tickles your nostrils. She clamps her hand over your mouth with her hand as the other two stuff you into the suit. None of it fits correctly. They handle you roughly, more like farmhands than ladies, except for when they smooth the suit over your body after dressing you. Three pairs of hands roaming your neck and chest, your shoulders. Your inseam, which embarrasses you.

Clara ties your left shirt sleeve in a knot, and your left jacket sleeve is stuffed into the left side pocket. As she finishes, the door opens and another voice—deeper, emptier, male—asks if they have any more guests to bring up. Clara says yes, and that they're dressing him now. The voice tells them to bring him upstairs, and the door shuts again.

The difference between "him" and "you" is one of vanity, isn't it?

An old woman rides her white bicycle down a bent, back country road surrounded by coarse farmland. There is little to break the monotony beyond scatterings of barns, grain silos, simple houses, and the occasional tuft of trees.

Further off, the green grass blackens around the isolated refineries that burn coal and shoot the steam through underground networks of pipes and channels to provide neighboring towns with electric power. Further off still are the mines, big excavations full of men pulling that coal from the cold, dark belly of the earth. It is hard, lonely work, something the old woman knows a lot about.

She steers her bicycle off the road and down a hill sloping away from it, stopping at a pile of stones. A man, clearly a coal miner, lays dead nearby. She kneels down and pulls a coin from behind his left ear, then stands again and drops the coin into her skirts.

With that done, the old woman remounts her bicycle and returns to the road, stopping to let a coal truck rattle past, its flatbed full of coal to be processed. She would come upon a house, her next destination, in due time.

The billiard room must be in the basement of a house, because the women lead you up a set of narrow stairs before removing your blindfold in an entrance hall of sorts.

Left to a competent staff, the room wouldn't be out of place in an ostentatious plantation home. The floor is creamy marble, and two staircases spin up to a landing with a sturdy balustrade and pots of flowers resting on half-columns. The undertrousers hanging over the balustrade diminish its grand effect, however.

That isn't the worst of it. The paintings on the walls are all crooked and scribbled on with oil crayons, or used as a target for eggs and long darts. Cards have been scattered across the floor, and coats have been piled near the front door, where a coat rack might have stood. A red stain runs down the bottom of the right-hand staircase. You can't tell if it is wax or paint or blood.

The doors to the left and right of you are shut, but you can hear voices and laughter, and that pernicious smoke smell hangs in the air like a bog mist. Clara pauses to repack the bong, and then you are led, or gently forced, up the left staircase and through a convoluted series of hallways and rooms.

Much of the house is poorly lit by overhead bulbs and gas lamps in brass wall fixtures. The narrower hallways are hot, the walls warm to the touch, most likely from steam coursing through a whole capillary system of pipes inside the walls.

You hear many voices as you navigate the house's dizzying passageways. Following them to their source would be impossible; the noise surrounds you on all sides, like water. Clara stops to listen to them a couple of times, but Beatrice and Alice will not be halted. They lead the way, while Clara guides you with a firm grip on your hand. She laces her fingers with yours, and her knuckles are as sharp as caltrops. Between that, the harsh dressing routine, your most-likely-broken nose, and the waning soreness in your ribs, aches sprout up in your body like vegetables after a rain.

As the four of you descend a staircase to an unlit landing, only to ascend another staircase for two stories, you wonder if they are in fact leading you away somewhere quiet and dark to kill you.

At the top of that second staircase, Beatrice pushes open one final door and holds it open for the rest of you. Voices rush out as the doors open, giving the impression that a party is being thrown in the room behind them.

A man shoves past Beatrice and steps out into the hallway. He is pale, wearing a high-collared shirt and vest, his undershorts, and black socks held to his legs with garters. A pair of suspenders has been stuffed into his vest pocket. One end dangles out. His top lip is split by a gap that reaches up into his nose, exposing the architecture of his front teeth. He hails the women by name, and seems wary of them.

The women explain, passing their bong among them in turn, that you are a guest to be admitted to the party at once, and push you through the doorway. You stumble into a large, gloomy parlor where paintings and stuffed animal heads hang on the walls. The other guests present, men and women alike, make no effort to welcome you or even notice your entrance.

You turn to the women who brought you here, but they are gone.

The old woman reached the house at exactly the moment she needed to, and has made her way inside. She passed unseen through a crowd of rough-looking party guests and sneered at the messes they made. They left glasses and cups and even clothing wherever they fell, and had defaced much of the interior decoration. Many of them seemed disoriented from the house's low light and confusing layout, which the old woman came to understand as she passed through sets of rooms that tumbled in and out of one another with no sense of logic.

Now, having found the thick wooden door she sought, weariness overtakes her, and she slaps herself across the face. She cannot sleep. Not yet.

It has been so long since she slept. So, so long.

The door leads into a servant's bedroom outfitted with a canopy bed, dresser, and a self-contained shaving station on wheels. Two large windows would have looked out onto the property, had they not been painted black.

One corpse is sprawled out on the bed, the other on the floor near the windows. The old woman takes coins from them. From their complexions and the expressions frozen on their faces, they clearly died from exhaustion.

A tray of food is rotting on the night table; half a roasted chicken, some cheese, and a bottle of old tokay. The woman on the floor has black paint under her fingernails, and left scratches behind on the windows.

Sudden noises from some unseen part of the house startle the old woman. Thankful to leave, she closes the door after herself, but does not lock it.

The room you've entered is one of exhausted refinement. The guests, no fewer than twenty men and women, are in evening dress: top coats, long white gloves, starched collars and ascots. Your own vaguely military attire makes you a better fit for this company than you would have been otherwise.

Tables dressed in white linens hold steaming silver trays of food and rows of champagne flutes, with bottles of champagne standing nearby in ice buckets. In stark contrast to their attire, the guests eat directly from the trays with their hands, chewing loudly and sucking their fingers. The rows of unused champagne flutes make more sense when you see them drinking directly from the bottles.

A string trio of violin, viola, and cello has been set up in one corner. They are playing through a light, airy arrangement that doesn't suit the mood of the room at all.

Other guests, more alert than the others, are stocking the tables with fresh food and drink. They are all men, all wearing blue jackets.

"Excuse me," you say to one of them, his complexion almost orange. "Where am I? What is this place?"

"A party," the man says, "thrown by a very hospitable gentleman. He'll want to see you enjoying yourself."

"Can you help me find the door?" you ask. "I don't think I should be here."

"Were you raised in a barn?" He shoves you, and you consider answering him in kind until you see two other men in blue jackets staring you down. "You can go when you've been dismissed. You'd know that if you had any manners. Go back to the party and stop bothering me."

Not knowing where else to go, you survey the refreshments table. The food in the trays is indiscernible, covered with a thick, pungent red sauce. You decide against eating, at least for now. As another guest takes your place at the trays to shovel food into his mouth, you move over to the champagne.

Of course you do. You never had the hand-to-eye coordination or physical grace for sports, nor the bullish confidence for games of chance. As a seducer of women, you were substandard at best. There is but one other way in which a man can take measure of himself, isn't there?

Your appetites for the grape and the leaf aroused no shortage of reverence from your contemporaries. They used to say you had a "hollow leg." All of you would go out carousing, but one by one they would all pull away from the bar and stumble home. Sometimes you would drink clear until morning, sweating and stinking as the sun rose at your back.

Four or five glasses muffle your various aches and bruises enough to make you more comfortable, and you introduce yourself to a tall, rangy gentleman in a green suit and gray vest. When you ask his name, he seems confused by the question. Pressing further, you learn that his name is Robinson, and that his breath reeks of liquor. He has a somnolent face and, as he sways in and out of the light, an untreated rash creeps up from his neck to his jawline.

Taking your leave of him, you attempt conversation with some of the other guests, to no avail. They seem confused, staring vacantly past one another, their faces and lapels

stained with food. Most hold drinks in their hands.
"What is a skeleton?" asks a round man in mismatched
jacket and trousers. His voice flat.

"Oh, I love this one," says a lady standing on unsteady
legs behind him.

"It's a lot of bones with the people scraped off," he says,
then wheezes out an attempt at laughter. The woman
behind him follows suit; her efforts are similarly joyless.
Moments later, you watch another man shove a handful
of meatballs into his mouth and stand there chewing,
crumbs of meat spilling down his chin. His eyes are
swollen and pink, his breathing labored.

Across the room, a short, thickly-built woman sips
champagne and you almost rush over to her. Of course
you do.

"Excuse me," you ask her. "What is this place?"

She laughs, her voice detuned by liquor. "Oh, you're fun!
I haven't talked to a new arrival in some time now." She
is wearing an elegant blue dress that exposes her large
shoulders. Her hair is done up like foreign royalty. "Have you
tried the food yet? The Count spares no expense on that."
She traces the rim of her champagne flute with a finger and
gestures to the musicians. "Or the entertainment. After a
while it's easy to forget they're still playing."

"How long is a while?" you ask.

"A week?" she says, after a moment of thought. "Maybe not so long. I don't remember when I arrived, exactly."

You did not expect that answer and it must have shown on your face, because a smile flashes across hers. She is missing some teeth. The ones left behind are yellow and twisted. "The Count's parties are open-ended," she says. She wipes her upturned nose with her bare hand.

"Who is the Count?" you ask. "Is this his house?"

"He was just here," the woman says, looking around. "He's a bit of a butterfly at these things. Can't hardly sit him still." She crosses the room and you follow her. Behind you, the musicians play with grim determination, slumped in their chairs, their skin glazed with old sweat.

There is something off about this woman, and not in a way that drink or fatigue would explain. Her movements are jerky, as though she is still learning them. When she gets drawn into another conversation that doesn't include you, you return to the refreshments table.

This house, as far as you can tell, is a honeycomb of separate parlors, with doors connecting them to their neighbors in all directions. The few windows you've seen have all been painted black. You ramble in and out of rooms, each full of food and drink and bleary-eyed glares from the vagrant guests leering and gibbering in them. Words gnarl and twist from their drooling mouths. Their laughter streaks the air with dust.

Have another drink. Your knees can hardly bend, your eyelids are heavy as leadshot, and yet you stand. You blink. You take refreshments as they are offered to you, which is whenever you're close to falling asleep.

Plates of spoiled food occupy the furniture of the room you stand in now. The carpet has been torn up to expose the floorboards. A circle has been carved into the floor, and a star within that, the points ornamented with runic symbols you can't identify.

"Wonder what that is," you say to an older man dressed for the safari. He shrugs, then coughs and spits.

"One of the Count's secrets," he says. "Whole place is full of 'em."

"I haven't run into the Count yet," you say. "Perhaps I'll ask him about it. Do you know where he is?"

The old man shakes his head and staggers away. Your attention is drawn to a skull mounted on the wall, similar to one you'd seen before. It is small, with oversized antlers that look out of place.

"What sort of animal is that?" you ask a gentleman in a herringbone overcoat and matching trousers.

"A jackalope," the man said. You've never heard of such a thing, and tell him so.

"They're the bastard sons of Coal Country," the man says, wiping his reedy mustache on his sleeve. "Part rabbit, part antelope."

"Is it yours?" you ask, pointing to the skull.

"Oh no, I've never managed to bag one for myself," the man says. "That's part of the Count's collection."

"Who is this Count?" There's no need to yell. "Where is he?"

"He'll come around," the man says. "He always does. This is a big house and he has to make the rounds." He turns to you, and his mournful face sends a jolt up your spine.

Why is that, now? Does he look like a union man, joined with his fellows outside a factory or meeting hall, demanding fair wages and humane conditions? Is his the face of a man who would run as the scabs and factory bulls piled out of those steam-trucks, or would his chin rise to meet their violence?

It is a face you would have left broken on the ground either way.

The old woman leans her white bicycle against a sturdy wooden bookshelf. The room she stands in has been outfitted with oil lamps obscured by purple glass, casting strange light on the walls and ceiling, which are all shelves.

The ceiling shelves are most impractical. As she looks around, a thick volume falls out of them and almost lands on her head. She picks it up and finds it to be an untranslated copy of Friedrich von Junzt's *Unaussprechlichen Kulten*. A few pages from the end matters are missing.

She puts it back where it landed and examines some of the other books along the wall shelves. They are old, and their spines are broken. Books are very human in this respect.

As she explores this library, the door is thrown open by an older man with thick eyebrows and the impudent grin of a drunkard. He wears an expensive, tailored dinner jacket, smart black boots, and nothing else. His dark hair has been mussed, and his build is heavy in that glutinous way that comes with overindulgence.

"You clean him up!" he yells out into the hallway. "You clean that son of a bitch up and you tell him that—hey, you see this jacket?" He tugs on a lapel as he stands in the doorway, fully exposed to whomever the other party is.

"This jacket cost more than any house he's ever lived in. You tell him that."

With that, the man slams the door and stomps through the library to a leather armchair sitting in a corner formed by two bookshelves. The old woman watches his footsteps fade from the dense carpet. By the time she opens the door to leave, the man has fallen asleep in the chair.

Following instincts bestowed upon her alone, the old woman leaves the room and descends two staircases to the dead, mangled body of another man in formal dress. Unlike the man asleep in the library, this one looks and smells like a vagrant, and has very obviously been beaten to death. The old woman bends and takes his coin from behind his ear, as she will do thousands of times more that day, curtly and without feeling.

As you wander, the rules are made plain to you, both by observation and by the men in blue jackets; eat, when offered. Drink, when offered. Do not fall asleep. No sudden movements. At the center of it all is the Count, and the stories of him darting madly around his mansion, plying his guests with food and drink, his concern that they "have fun" sounding more and more sinister. You imagine a man with blood-swept strings flowing from his fingers to the limbs of his guests. Perhaps he is imagining that same thing.

The guests here have no shortage of deformities—misshapen bodies, rashes, warts, goiters, skin discolorations, exposed tattoos—and yet you are the only one here with a missing limb. Other guests touch it, ask you about it, call attention to it with loud, mocking comments. You are a weird little curiosity for them to marvel at, the one-armed vagrant putting on airs in upmarket clothes. It's hard not to feel as though a leper's bell hangs around your neck.

You tell everyone who asks that you lost the arm in a war, and that those memories are still too raw to discuss. You are lying, of course.

Meanwhile, you see the women who brought you here at odd intervals—as convex reflections in spoons, in shadows cast by other guests in erratic gaslight, as footprints in the carpet. Are they following you? No. Impossible. You're not worthy of surveillance.

The old woman walks among the coins.

The rows of shelves bend at sharp angles, the ledgers in them a flat, unbroken line. Each spine bears a capital letter in gold leaf. The filing system was designed for a boundless memory. The woman pulls ledgers out and opens them, running her hands along the coins pasted onto squares of stiff black board. Each coin-bearer's name is written in silver script under his or her coin. One by one, she sorts the coins from her skirts into their proper sleeves.

The coins demand this level of reverence in their storage. Every man, woman, and child is issued a coin. It is their life essence, their sense of self, a functional neuroimage around which the bearers' path through life takes shape. Most coins are shared from one being to the next, worn down and cleaned and passed along until they can no longer be reused, at which point they are annealed and restruck. Repurposed coins are replaced by wooden duplicates.

The old woman knows each coin, and the life of its bearer, by its abrasions and bag marks. She has seen them walk under cherry blossom trees in spring and build crackling fires in winter. She has watched them grow old, die, be forgotten. The shiniest and newest coins in the collection depress her the most.

Sometimes the old woman doesn't look at the coins at all. She looks at the negative space between them, tracing the concave diamond shapes made between the coins' round edges.

In a small parlor covered in maps, most of them outdated, you find Clara pouring champagne into glasses. Alice and Beatrice stand near steaming trays of food; the latter keeps an eye on the room as the former packs crumbs of marijuana into the bowl of that ominous black glass bong. Their kinetic presence is jarring in comparison to the guests'. They urge everyone to eat and drink freely, and when a sick-looking man in academic tweeds reaches for a fork, they tell him to eat with his hands.

When Clara sees you, she flashes a smile and beckons you over. "Are you having fun?"

"I don't know," you say, reaching for some champagne. "None of this makes any sense."

Clara's smile hardens. "What do you mean?"

"Are you joking?" You're starting to yell again. "I woke up nude in your basement, you forced me into these clothes, and shoved me into this party full of drunk vagrants who won't shut up about my—" Your voice breaks. "My arm. What is this place, and who are you?"

"There's no need to insult the others by calling them vagrants," Clara says. Alice and Beatrice appear on either side of you.

"You three abducted me from the street," you say. "I can only assume the others were taken the same way. I know vagrants when I see them, and these are vagrants." Stop yelling. You're making a fool of yourself and splashing champagne everywhere. "Now either tell me what the hell is happening here or let me go home."

Beatrice grips your shoulder. "He wants to meet the Count, does he?" She smiles.

"We should throw him down the stairs for being such an ingrate," Alice says.

"No no," Beatrice says, as you consider running away. "If he wants to meet the Count, let's give him a proper introduction."

Clara smiles and links arms with you as Beatrice and Alice lead you into a room filled with warped and broken mirrors. Some kind of crude dancing lesson is being held in here, to the tune of three musicians playing accordion, kick drum, and cello. At the center of the room is an older man in a tailored dinner jacket and red trousers. His dark hair and eyebrows suggest grooming, and his beery smile suggests mischief, but not vacancy. A foul-smelling cheroot smolders in his hand as he leads a blond woman in a mechanized waltz, well out of time with the accompaniment.

"Dance, everyone!" he bellows, breaking away from his partner to shove the others into reticent pairs. "Come on! Dance to this lovely music!" He watches them lurch to the music, then returns to the blond woman, who slips out of his arms and runs away. She leaves an elbow-length glove bunched in the crook of his elbow.

The man is offended by her refusal and ends the dance lesson abruptly, at which point Clara waves him over.

"One of your guests has asked for an audience with you," she says to him, nudging you.

He extends his hand. "Charmed," he says. "I am Count Drogado."

You were taught as a boy that the first thing a man knows of you is your handshake. You give the Count a firm one on instinct, which he does not expect. His father never taught him that, you suppose.

"Are you enjoying yourself, sir?" he asks, withdrawing his hand. "I pride myself on being a good host."

"If that's the case," you say, "you can start by telling me where I am, exactly."

"My house," the Count says. "One of them, anyway. This is my Coal Country estate, as it were." He pauses, interrupted by shrill laughter from elsewhere in the room.

"You dragged me all the way out to Coal Country?" you ask. As far as Coal Country stretches across the map, it's still miles away from the city.

The Count smirks. "What do you mean, 'dragged you here'? I didn't drag anyone anywhere."

"Well, they did the dragging," you say, pointing to the women as they pass the bong between them, blowing smoke into a communal cloud that spreads across the room. "But the effect is still the same."

"Watch your tone, friend," the Count says, trying to appear haughty instead of frustrated. "And watch how you talk about my wives. I've entertained generals, kings, and presidents in this house. You're lucky to be here. This," he says, gesturing across the room, "is where the action is."

You watch Alice, Beatrice, and Clara smoke. So that's who they are. "I've had enough action for one evening," you say, "or however long I've been trapped in here. I'd like to take my leave."

"What's the matter?" the Count asks. "Gotta go home and help the missus clean dishes? I'm extending an invitation to all the food, drink, and merriment you could ever want." He throws an arm around your shoulders.

"And all I ask is that you stay a while longer."

"I wasn't invited," you say, ducking out from under his arm. "I was abducted."

The Count's jaw stiffens. "You wouldn't be here if you weren't invited. Now, we've just set down more refreshments. Have a bite and think about your options here."

"I'm not hungry," you say.

The Count slaps the table hard enough to startle his wives and draw the rest of the room's attention. "Ladies! Gentlemen! Our new guest isn't hungry!" His announcement is met with drowsy jeers. "Or so he says. I think he just needs a taste to stoke his appetite."

At that moment, you are seized. A man in a blue jacket jams his fat, dirty fingers into your mouth. You bite his fingers and yell as loud as you can, but more hands pull your mouth open and shove food inside. You kick at your assailants until you are forced to your knees so more food can be stuffed down your gullet. A horrid mix of crackers and cheese and meat. Wet, stringy vegetables.

Everywhere, hands. Forcing you to chew, fingers bruising your throat to make you swallow, knees and elbows boring into your back and legs. Their laughter turns to mush in your ears. Tears burn in your eyes. The Count swings his arms to and fro, as though conducting an orchestra. His mouth is a distended ribbon of teeth. He holds a glass of champagne to your lips and you drink it to wash down some of the food. He smiles as you drink and turns away once you are let loose and thrown on the ground.

"Everyone!" he exclaims. "Let's reconvene in the next room and give the musicians a break, eh?" He slaps the cellist on the shoulder. "My brides will lead us in some parlor games in the meantime."

The guests lurch into the next room in a single, practiced motion as you choke and cough. You spit a dandelion onto the floor. It leaves a bitter taste on your tongue.

Look at yourself running.

You are a knot of digesting food, eyes hot with tears. Your feet ache in the ill-fitting boots you were given, and you press your back against the door to kick them off and away down the staircase you've found. It is unlit, dropping into a yawning emptiness.

You waited until the Count's back was turned and ran from that room. One of the blue-jacketed chaperons hollered after you, but did not pursue. As you start down the stairs, newly barefoot, you step on a square of billiards chalk.

Patches of light shaped like small windows cringe in the gloom. You hurry down the stairs as the sounds of oppressive merriment fade behind you. You've found a corner of the house modeled after the dungeons laid out in penny dreadfuls. Dripping water, moist walls, utter darkness anywhere the windows don't reach.

Spit, laden with chunks of food, forces itself up into your mouth. You cough it out behind you, hear it splatter on the cold wooden step.

You have seen men cast into worse than this. Standing outdoors all day waiting to be chosen as brute labor, at the mercy of sun and rain, stirred even the most genial among you to violence. At first, you all fought each other. Then the unionists began their agitations, and you were cordial to them until you saw the factory bulls cast them into the cabins of steamtrucks. You have seen their bodies cowhided with bruises and welts. You ran from those fields, those wide cobblestone thoroughfares, those gravel lots pooling out and around the entrances of coal mines as the trucks scuffed away.

You used to drink more then, not to gain courage, but to numb cowardice. You ran then, and you run now. How dare you.

The staircase ends at a narrow landing and splits. You
break right, and the stairs narrow as you descend. You
stumble, regain yourself, and proceed from there as if on
a tightrope, placing one trembling foot directly in front
of the other. Your lungs and throat feel like burlap as you
cough up more food. You can still taste the hands that
forced open your mouth.

The stairs end in a narrow hallway that widens as you
pass through another door. You hear human voices again.
Your heart rages in your chest, a bird trapped in the
chimney of your body. It is the last wild part of yourself.
The rest is all soot.

The old woman pulls ledgers and folders out, slipping the
coins she has collected into their assigned sleeves. Many
of these will be reassigned to new bearers. They're not in
bad shape.

"I wonder if any of you knew this was going to happen,"
she says, running her hand across a page of coins. A
common belief among the living is the idea that souls are
precious, unique, specific to their bearer. It would break
them to learn that souls are a resource to be recycled and
destroyed, like everything else.

She had taken coins from the ears of the dead in seaside villages traversable only by canals swollen with garbage, and from boomtowns in sandy deserts where oil had been struck, and from strange cities where the streets were paved with magnetic glass.

There were thousands of coins to be filed away, and the following day would bring thousands more. If time were actually linear or circular, instead of the rotating cube she knows it to be, her task would be impossible. But time is a cube, and she pedals her bicycle along its harmonic corners every day, appearing in thousands of separate locations in the space of an instant.

"There now," she says to the ledger she's holding. "Everyone comfortable in there?" She slides it back into place on the shelf, then jingles the coins in her skirts. "Hope you lot have better luck this next go-around."

She settles her skirts and rubs her forehead. "This is why I need a cat around here. Talking to a bunch of coins like a crazy person. I lose my mind in here some days."

Once she finishes cataloging her coins for the day, the old woman traces the outline of a cat in the dust covering one especially old ledger. After a moment of thought, she draws a second cat, and crosses their tails before returning the ledger to its place.

The idleness has set in. Numb from lack of sleep,
you collapse on the floor of a long hallway. The wall
to your right has been outfitted with large windows
that have not been painted over, and look out onto a
generous expanse of property. The land is marshy and
dappled brown, stretching out farther than you can see
from this vantage point.

Idleness is what your father called these periods of fatigue
where you slept for days and sat still in the dark when
you were awake. He told you that it was immoral to
lose interest in the everyday, that it would ruin you and
already had. To be able-bodied and resist work was a sign
of evil, he thought, and his remedy was to work the devil
out of you, or failing that, to chase it out with a leather
belt. That belt drove you from the house as surely as your
own feet.

You could never explain what brought on the waning
energy and lack of motivation, or the accompanying
feelings of worthlessness. Even when you smiled and
sang like every other boy your age, those feelings
hummed along underneath, capable of resurfacing at
any moment. Then it was the plow and the hot sun and
the strap, and tears just beyond the glow of the fires
your father set at night.

That idleness never really went away, did it? It crept back into your heart during the transition from rural farm life to the impersonal city. There was no comfortable medium to be found anywhere. Your feet ached from walking on cobblestones and hard pavement with no clear idea of where you were, panicking as people filled the streets all at once, in every direction.

Finding work in the city, you learned, was a humiliating public lottery. You and the other unemployables would gather in public lots, hoping to be hired by factory or mill foremen for day wages. Sometimes you were, sometimes not. Remaining unchosen in a crowd of men just like you is a unique and crushing loneliness. Even among your peers, you are insignificant. It got harder to convince yourself to care at all, after a while, and the only thing that numbed your swelling angst was liquor.

Then you lost your arm.

You're nothing. You've always been nothing. With your arm gone, you're even less. Every time your father fired one of his farmhands, he would say "vessels that can't carry water get thrown back into the fire." You think about that a lot.

You must have dozed off, because you don't notice Count Drogado staggering naked down the hallway until he throws his jacket on you.

"Hey!" you see him yell down the hall. "Don't act like you're not interested in getting to know the man of the house! I'm the best thing to happen to women since the underbust corset!"

You look around the corner to see that he has discarded his shoes and socks as well. You hear other noises too, muffled human voices that are either laughing or crying out in great pain.

Skirts ruffle behind you, and you turn around to see that Clara has knelt beside you. Her eyes and nose are obscured by her hair, but she has a heart-shaped face underneath, and a way of pursing her lips into a smile that holds your attention.

"You look lonely," she says, clasping both of her hands around yours. "And tired."

You nod, your bent legs at an uncomfortable angle . You turn the stump of your left arm to the wall. One of her hands slides across to your left shoulder. Her reedy fingers bend around the arc of your stump. Her bong rests at her feet. Lipstick is smudged around the mouthpiece.

"Come play a game with me," she says.

You rise to your feet when she does, and follow her into a room whose walls are blotted with nicotine stains and covered with strange symbols. Crude paintings of serpents and skulls and five-pointed leaves. An oil crayon portrait of a nun, naked except for her wimple, rising out of a vulgarly-drawn flower. There is an animal skull just over the door frame. It has antlers, but the skull is too small to belong to a deer or moose. An *X* has been drawn between its eyes in red paint.

You join six other guests in various stages of fatigue, and Clara has you all form a circle in the center of the room. "We're going to play blind man's bluff," she says through

a puff of smoke. "And this gentleman is going first." She squeezes your shoulder.

"I don't understand any of this," you say, as she lowers a blindfold over your eyes. You let her do this. Once the blindfold is secured, all you can see is cornsilk cloth and hushed light, leaving you vulnerable for a fist in your ribs. Your knees buckle and you cry out.

"Now count to ten," Clara says. "Everyone else, don't let him catch you!"

Once you reach ten, you stumble around the room waving your arm around, trying to grab the other players. You can feel your pulse in your eyelids. The other players' footfalls are heavy and clumsy, but you can't quite gauge their distance from you. You fall to your knees twice before you finally grab another player, and bump into the furniture a few times before finding a second. You imagine leaving big sweaty pawprints on them, like a dog, and wonder if they see your shoulder bucking up and down inside your jacket. Your missing arm is searching for them, too.

When you find Clara, she calls "time!" and pulls off your blindfold. To your horror, you find your hand pressed firmly to her bosom, with her hand holding yours there.

"You only found three of us," she says, playfully scolding you. "I think you can do better next time." She releases your hand and goes to put the blindfold on someone else. The two players you found are slumped against the wall, clutching their stomachs as blood soaks through their clothes. Alice is standing in the doorway, and leaves just as you turn to face her, letting the door shut behind her. She was holding a knife, you think.

You hurry from the room.

The old woman stands in the doorway with her white bicycle. Every line in her tapered face is crisp. Her nails dig into the rubberized grip on the bicycle's handlebars. She is early.

She watches Mr. Robinson wilt into a chair near a window in the far corner of an empty room. The tables and a large pot of ice have been overturned and left to seep into the carpet. Three of the room's wall-mounted gas lamps have been upset. They leak down the room's wood-paneled walls. Only a bookshelf laden with curios has gone undisturbed.

Robinson is sweating. His extremities tremble. Another door opens and two men in blue jackets enter the room. They hold the door open for Count Drogado, who surveys the mess and clucks his tongue. A long, thin squeak escapes Robinson's throat.

"Come join the party, Mr. Robinson," the Count says, his voice heavy. His clothes and hair are disheveled, and he holds onto the back of a chair for support.

"Let me open the window," Robinson says, pawing at the brass latch holding it shut. "I need some air."

"You're just tired," Drogado says. "Come on, friend. I'll make you a drink. It'll wake you right up."

"I've had enough," Robinson says. "Please. Just let me get some air."

The Count cracks his knuckles against his leg, which makes the old woman wince. "I think I'll know when you've had enough." He advances on Robinson, who springs out of the chair with the last of his strength. He falls in the marsh of spilled food and drink, sprawls out in it. His throat and nostrils burn.

"Why do you keep me here?" Robinson asks. "Any of us? What is wrong with you, old man?"

"What's wrong with me?" the Count yells, pulling him up by his collar, ripping it. He slaps Robinson across the face. "What's wrong with me is that I came from a world made of men, and we crushed weak little insects like you under our feet!" Veins in the Count's neck bulge as he slaps Robinson again, and again, finally throwing him to the ground and stomping him.

At times like this, the old woman really wishes she had the power to intervene.

"I've spent more money on spilled liquor than you've ever seen!" the Count yells. "Do you hear me? I've opened a door for you, and everyone else here, into the kind of luxury you've only dreamed about! And you're telling me you just want some air?"

The Count exhausts himself and sits in Robinson's chair near the window. Robinson lays in a heap, surrounded by trash. A slow wheeze rolls out from his lungs. Drogado snaps his fingers, and the two men in blue jackets grab the bookcase on either side and drag it closer to Robinson. Curios fall from the shelves as they maneuver it into position, then throw it down on top of Robinson. They pull it up and throw it down again, and again.

Drogado remains seated for a moment longer, then his legs get restless. "It's too quiet in here," he says to the men

in blue jackets. "I need more people around. Let's keep this going."

After Drogado leaves, the old woman walks over to Robinson and lifts the bookcase with one hand, giving herself just enough room to kneel and pluck a coin from behind his ear. His coin rattles alongside the others in her skirts, which come up stained red where they cover her knees.

Further up the hall, you see Alice open a door and disappear. You follow her into a modest parlor where twelve other guests stand around refreshment tables, drinking beer and eating oysters from cast iron pots. Wall mounted lights and an overhead bulb give the room a warm glow that has been absent elsewhere in the house. The air in this room smells strongly of butter and onions.

The guests all talk among themselves in low, murmuring tones, punctuated by ripples of argument and sour laughter. It is not a friendly crowd. As you help yourself to a beer, the room's clear light reveals them to be nothing short of cadaverous. Their clothes are mottled and stained, showing wear as if they'd been lived in for days, and their teeth are visible through their sunken cheeks.

Alice appears with a large serving bowl and drops it on the table, directly in front of you. You back away as she tilts a bottle of brandy over the bowl, filling it up to the lip. Reaching into the cleft of her bosom, she pulls out a bag of raisins and empties it into the bowl as well. You and some of the others watch the raisins sink to the bottom.

"The name of this game," Alice says, after drawing deeply from her bong, "is snap-dragon. Who here has matches?" A tallowy gentleman with thick side-whiskers finds a box of them after patting himself down, and hands them to Alice. In so doing, his hand touches hers. You notice that.

Alice takes them and curtly nods her thanks. She has a wide face and a flat-bridged nose to match. Her lips bow into a natural frown, lined on either side with creases. She is more compact than her sisters, shorter and broader in a way that her white dress does not flatter.

Alice lights a match and drops it in the brandy. Blue flames spread across the bowl, their tips almost white. "Whoever gets the most raisins wins," she says.

"Wins what?" asks a ghoulish woman with skin like old soap.

"You'll see," Alice says. Her smile bares small white teeth.

One by one, all of you try reaching into the flames to pull a raisin out from them. Your hands snap back in turn. You try three times, wanting to impress Alice, and the third attempt sees a flame catch the cuff of your jacket. You beat your arm against your thigh to extinguish it and finish your beer. You pour yourself another.

Alice appears at your side and holds the bong's mouthpiece directly under your nose. You indulge her, then pass it back. She takes it without looking at you. Her eyes have found another, an impish man in a baggy morning-coat. He is steadying his hand over the flames. As other guests edge their hands to the fire and pull away, yelping and sucking on their singed fingers, this man acts with deliberation.

Back in your laboring days, you and a handful of layabouts trapped a feral cat in a cage to bet on the outcome of a fight between it and a large spider someone had found in an old boxcar. The cat won. You'd bet on the spider.

Alice grabs your hand and uses it to push the impish-looking man's hand, and your own, into the burning brandy. Your screams send the others reeling away from the bowl. You can't feel any raisins.

Instead of pulling your hand from the bowl right away, you leave it there, breathing hard through your clenched teeth, the pain raw and bright. The other man

is screaming, his hand trapped under yours. You look at
Alice with tears in your eyes, and for what? Approval?
You resolve to not let your hand out until she smiles
at you, no matter how much it hurts you or the man
struggling to free himself from your grotesque plea for
attention. It's not his fault you'll endure any punishment
as long as someone else is enduring worse.

Alice smirks at you and you pull your hand out. It's red,
and will blister. You find a bucket of ice that's mostly
water and submerge your hand, experiencing new and
different pain. The other man's hand has boiled down to
the meat. The hell with him, and the others. Let them
broadcast their horror and disgust on their ugly faces. As
they scatter, you look for Alice again. She is gone.

You're a monster, you know.

The old woman walks her bicycle down a set of stairs,
one step at a time. The stairs are swaddled in near-total
darkness, their ascent broken by landings, no doors or
hallways. Coins rattle in her skirts, and she pictures
herself stumbling and falling, then chasing after this
wealth of coins as they scatter and roll away in the dark.

She reaches a door and opens it with relief, walking her
bicycle down a short hallway, following a thin patina of

steam that thickens at a set of double doors. They swing into a cramped, stuffy kitchen. The cooks are dressed in filthy chef's whites and operating almost a dozen separate ovens, stoves, steamplates, and sauce-boilers. Between these appliances and the cooks' clanging and yelling, the room is a steady ocean of noise. Steam lathers up from every surface.

The old woman nudges past them, looking for the one with a coin to be collected. Their faces are flushed, drooping, their complexions coarse. The dead one leans against the wall next to a row of iceboxes. As the old woman takes his coin, cooks rush to a sliding window in waves, handing food to unseen servants to be taken to various rooms in the house. Someone tasting a sauce burns herself, screams. Another cuts himself chopping carrots four at a time. He sweeps them into a bowl, blood and all. Mold creeps up from a drain in the center of the floor, barely visible through the steam.

This will be the last one for today, the old woman decides as she leaves, humming a tune that time has since forgotten.

You hear a woman humming and chase the sound down a series of corridors that, to your gratitude, do not involve any more flights of stairs. The tapestries on the walls are gruesome displays of splayed-open goats and tangled limbs and men in black cloaks denouncing women who burn at stakes with bags over their heads.

The gentleman whose hand you burned is sitting on the floor, his back pressed against the wall. He's looking at you, not sure what to make of what just happened.

"So when did they get you?" he asks, before you can say anything. His eyes swell red in his pale face. "How long ago was it?"

"I don't know," you say.

The man almost laughs. "Why did you burn me back there?" He forces himself to his feet, his ruined hand tucked under his other arm.

"I didn't." Yes you did. You could have resisted.

"They took me right off the street," he says, not registering your response. "Knocked me out with a shock stick and dressed me in these." He sneers at his jacket and trousers.

You recall the steamcoach cornering you in the alley. Your stomach churns. "I'm sorry I burned you," you tell him.

"No, you aren't," he says. He's right. "Those women befoul the mind. I've done things in this house that sicken me." He shrinks into himself a little. "And leave me cold."

"What about the Count?" you ask.

"That man is not of this earth," he says. "He never sleeps, never tires of revels. How he hasn't drunk himself to death or smoked his bones hollow, I will never understand."

"Is he trying to kill us?"

"I don't know. Now I sound like you." The man leans against the wall, his fatigue obvious.

"They took me from an alley," you say. You thought it might feel good, or liberating, to say this. It doesn't. Your muscles are tense. "I'm sorry."

He turns away from you, not saying anything more. You walk past him and try the door at the end of the corridor. It is locked. You turn back and he is gone. His jacket is crumpled on the ground.

The old woman leans her bicycle against a mossy, time-worn gravestone in a small cemetery. Ahead, Count Drogado's house rises in mockery of the stormy sky above it. The rain that had accompanied this visit to the Count's estate—the first stop in her day's errands—has calmed itself down to flecks that weren't worth opening an umbrella.

Count Drogado himself is standing outside, his clothes soaked through with rain. His three brides are gathered around him. One of them tips a flask to his lips, and after a short volley of kisses, he retires to the house, leaving his three wives outside.

As the old woman gets closer, she sees a body at their feet, face-down on the ground. To her left is a barn with an attached, spindly-looking silo. Birds circle around the top, cawing at each other in what sounds almost like confusion. Out of curiosity, the old woman breaks from her errand and explores the barn, which holds a monstrous, rusting steam-baler and a wall of herbaceous plant bales. A thick, grassy scent hangs in the air, along with traces of sweet manure despite the absence of any horses.

With faint disappointment, the old woman leaves the barn and returns to her purpose there. The brides are still standing over the dead body. One of them turns him over with her foot.

"He looks like that coach driver the Count had when he was courting Clara," Beatrice says to Alice in between rips from the bong. "Remember him? Remember that stupid coach he drove?"

Alice laughs. "Trying to maneuver it down our little street, yes! He kept having to relight his parking lamps.

Just dreadful, the whole thing." She pauses to relight the bong; her voice has gotten scratchy.

"Nicest thing anyone ever did for that poor man was when I tossed him in front of that other coach that came roaring in behind us," she says, as the old woman plucks a coin from the dead man's ear. "Crushed him like a bug." She laughs again, louder this time. "His parking lamps were still lit!"

The other two laugh at this recollection. The old woman shakes her head and walks away, tucking the coin into her skirts.

"What did the Count say to that?" Beatrice asks. "I don't remember."

"Nothing," Alice says. "What could he say? The coach was taking up the whole street. The driver would never pass through, we all knew it. I did him the kindness of making it someone else's problem."

"He must have liked it," Beatrice says, referring to the Count. "He proposed to Clara the next day."

"Five days later, actually," Alice says.

Clara reaches into her skirts and pinches a small, white thing between her thumb and forefinger. "I kept one of his teeth," she says after taking the bong from Alice.

"When enough of mine fall out, I'll make it fit. It will be my gift to him."

Alice glares at her. "That's stupid," she says, and walks back into the house.

Beatrice puts her hand on Clara's shoulder. "It is stupid," she says, "but keep it anyway. You'll think of a better use for it."

The old woman watches them from her bicycle. She doesn't leave until the front door shuts behind them.

Sometimes you have dreams where you are shaking hands. Rows and rows of them, one after another. Endless fields of hands all knocking together like cornstalks in the breeze.

You wake up from one such dream to find Beatrice examining your shoulder, where your arm used to be. You jolt and roll away, but she catches you even as she draws deeply from her bong. She bares her teeth and you swallow against the knife blade she presses to your throat.

"How did it happen?" she asks, blowing smoke into your face.

"It was an accident," you tell her. "A stupid accident." This is the first time you've really seen her up close. Her face is too wide for her features to sit comfortably, and her hair clumps from her head like a knot of brown cobwebs. Night-colored circles ring her eyes, made even darker by her pale complexion. A new dandelion garland stretches across her forehead, and she adjusts it with her free hand, as though hiding something.

"Is that why you're so ashamed?" she says, applying more pressure with the blade. "Don't be. People are stupid accidents, and you're no different. Now answer my question."

"A surgeon removed it," you say. The blade at your throat bends your voice into something absurd. "It was a few years ago."

"Why?" Beatrice asks. Her flower garland slips down her forehead and a faint glow throbs under it. You hear sudden cries from distant rooms, then footsteps, then the cries get louder and more distinct as a group of revelers runs down the hall. You can't tell if they see what's happening to you. If they do, it doesn't stop them. One of them braces his hand against the wall and vomits, then staggers away after the others.

Beatrice's eyes have not left yours during this interlude, and once the hallway is empty again, she rocks the blade from side to side.

"I used to work in a textile workhouse," you say. "Have you ever done factory work?"

Beatrice shakes her head.

"Don't," you say. "It's awful. Long days, pounding heat, and the work is mindless. It's all paced by whistles. The only breaks we got were for meals and whenever the machinery overheated."

"What did you do when that happened?" Beatrice asks. Even as she holds a knife to your throat, you're flattered that she cares enough to ask.

"Smoked cigarettes, mostly. Played cards, usually euchre or stone-a-pig. There was a set of old metal tripods near the loading dock, so we used those to play horseshoes. Taught the kids how to play, too."

"How thoughtful," Beatrice says. You can't tell if she's being sarcastic or not.

"Well, they already knew how to smoke," you say.

"Never mind that," Beatrice says, pressing the blade down harder. "Get to the point."

"We all drank a lot, too," you say. "Didn't have much energy for anything else. It wears on a person, leads to mistakes, injuries. One man slipped and fell from an elevated catwalk, another accidentally stitched the fingers on his right hand together. I used to hear stories of children getting sucked into the turbines and gnashed in the gears. How the sound of their arm and thigh bones echoed across the floor when they snapped."

Beatrice's eyes practically gleam at this portion of your story. Her tongue snakes across her thin lips. "Did you ever hear it yourself?"

"Only my own arm," you say, pacing each word carefully.

"I was attending a drawing frame, which wasn't my normal workstation, and my shirt was too loose for it. It snagged my sleeve and dragged my arm in up to the shoulder." You pause and tilt your head as a bead of sweat rolls down your brow; you don't want it getting in your eyes. "I remember it being a popping sound, more than snapping."

Beatrice relieves some of the pressure on your throat as you tell her that you were given tincture of cannabis for the pain. "Two of the bulls tried to pull me out," you say, "but I was in too deep and threw the gears off their tracks."

"So how did they get you out?" Beatrice asks.

"Probably knocked me out with chloroform and hacked my arm off right there," you say. "That's how they handled it most of the time. All I remember is someone tying off the stump."

Beatrice laughs quietly, almost to herself. "When you die," she asks, "will you float up into the firmament where angels will graft your arm back on with their gossamer tears? Or will you just rot in the ground like a man who would have kept his arm if his shirt had fit properly?"

"I don't know," you say. Of course you don't know. Your motivation for learning left when your arm did, in a pocket of time that was both an instant and an aeon of light-bending pain and regret. You look away from Beatrice, who is still laughing. You haven't finished your story, but you have nothing left to say. An insect crawls across the floor and you watch it slip into a crack between the floor and the wall.

"Can you still feel your arm?" Beatrice asks.

"Not so much anymore," you say. "I used to feel it a lot. Sometimes it—" you grit your teeth. "The stump would jerk around without me wanting it to, but that doesn't happen any more."

"Sounds like you've forgotten it," Beatrice says.

"More the other way around," you say.

Beatrice drags the knife away and stands up. When you

make no motion to do the same, she leaves. You stare up at the ceiling until the stinging in your throat fades away, and you don't feel much of anything at all.

Eventually, you find yourself in a crowded drawing room. Everywhere you stand seems to be in the way of someone else pushing past you for refreshments. You don't know where to arrange yourself, or who to talk to, and you end up downing three pots of beer just to quiet your head.

A crowd has gathered around a long banquet table with cups in billiard formation on either end. The group seems to be halved into teams, engaged in a game wherein they bounce a celluloid ball down the table, trying to land it in the other team's cups. You watch their reflections in a grand, gilt-frame mirror on the wall opposite them, but can't make sense of the game or the drinking that occurs at irregular, but purposeful, intervals.

It seems like every time you breathe, more people appear in the room, spilling beer on their finery and lighting cigarettes with unsteady hands. Another game has broken out behind you; a circle of consumptive-looking drunks blow at a feather to keep it in the air.

After two more pots of beer, you ask to be let into the ball-and-cups game occupying the banquet table. You have to shout over the other players to be understood.

A scowling fireplug of a woman tells you no, then grabs your empty jacket sleeve. "Hey!" she yells, as three of her compatriots giggle at you. "You playing pocket billiards in there?" She tugs at your sleeve. "Can we play too?" Their faces swell with malice as the woman yanks on your sleeve. The exposure of your shoulder stump sends them into gales of hideous laughter. For a moment, you want to smash this woman's nose.

Would you strike a woman? Very little is beneath you. You choose instead to sulk away from her mockery.

As you leave the table, you accidentally back into a different woman and find that you've crushed her folding paper fan. You try to apologize, but she sneers at you. You cannot hear what she is saying, but it seems unkind. One of her eyes wanders to the left. Her cheeks and nose are an alcoholic blush.

Someone else grabs you and it's Clara. She pulls you off to another corner of this massive room, where Beatrice and Alice wait for her with ten other guests. Alice is bent over their glass bong. Smoke fogs up the neck of it as she inhales.

"We are going to play Hot Boiled Beans," Alice says, clapping her hands with excitement. "The rules are simple. We select a person to be 'It,' and then an object. The person who is 'It' closes their eyes, and we have until the count of ten to hide the object. Whoever is 'It' has to find it, and the rest of the group gives them hints by yelling 'hot' if they're close to finding it, and 'cold' if they aren't. Does everyone understand?"

The group murmurs in agreement, which rankles Alice. She stomps on a random woman's foot hard enough to break the woman's shoe and produce a howl from her. "Does everyone understand?" she repeated.

This time, the crowd response is louder.

"Now, to pick something to hide." Alice looks around, removing a man's spectacles, a woman's broach, pulling another man's false teeth from his mouth and throwing them to the ground. Finally, she settles on Beatrice's dandelion garland, and slowly unwinds it from her head. Beatrice looks almost nude without it.

A third eye, set into Beatrice's forehead, has been exposed. It makes a triangle with her two primary eyes and glows in this parlor's somber lighting. All the spit leaves your mouth and all the air leaves your body.

"Now who's going to be It?" Alice asks. No one volunteers. She drags you into the center of what is becoming a circle. You notice that one of her hands is blistered and discolored.

"This is Thomas and he's going to be It!" Alice says. She clasps her hands over your eyes and asks everyone to count to ten. They do, their voices a staggering, drunken choir.

"No, please, I don't..." you say, but your protests are ignored.

At *eight*, Alice pokes you right in the eye.

At *ten*, she yells "Hot boiled beans and bacon for supper, hurry up before it gets cold!" and uncovers your eyes. Black spots float around in your vision. Beatrice's third eye blinks and swivels in its vertical socket. It must be a trick of the light, or a masterful illusion.

As you recall, you're supposed to find whatever the group hid, and they're supposed to yell out degrees of "hot" and "cold," depending on how close you are to the hidden item. In a daze, you walk over to a hutch and pull open the glass-fronted cabinet doors, looking for Beatrice's flower garland. You pull random knickknacks out of the hutch until you hear "cold."

You move on, pulling the cushions from an armchair and reaching into the cracks. You find a ring, crusted red on the inside of the shank, but no flowers. "Cold!" is the verdict from the group. Some of them laugh at you as you pull up the Oriental rug.

You're getting angry. You never were a good sport, especially after a few drinks. You throw the chair's seat cushion onto the ground and kick it. One of the others tells you to calm down and you shout at him, jab him in the chest with your finger. He's too drunk to care and wanders away.

Clara clears her throat and you turn to see all three women smiling, with their hands behind their backs. It can't be that easy. You tear through a sidepiece full of silverware while what's left of the group yells "Cold! Cold!"

You get warm when you approach Clara, who doesn't struggle when you pull her hands from behind her back. They are empty.

Beatrice holds out her empty hands as you approach. She locks all of her eyes with yours as an empty beer pot shatters the gilt-framed mirror. You once watched a crab thrash out from its shell to find another and that's how you feel now, in Beatrice's three-eyed gaze. You cannot return it for long, and turn away in disgust.

"Warmer!" someone yells from behind you. Muttering follows. You turn and stare at the rest of the players. Stupid and heavy, they are, in the second-hand formals that wax and wane from their scabrous bodies. They look like the other drunks you would park yourself among, drowning your sorrows after leaving an open labor call with no job. That is to say, they look like you. Drunk, filthy, mangled by the teeth of that imperial crusher of blood and flesh that is the modern city.

You feel hands on your shoulder stump. Clara's hands, yet again. You pull away and she pulls you back. "Such an unusual shape," she says. "Like a flipper, or a fin. Yes, a fish's fin." She smiles, bares teeth.

"Please, stop," you tell her.

"Why are you ashamed of it?" she asks. "Amputations are so..." She searches for the word. "Commonplace."

She doesn't know that you're the one who ran away from home, who came to the city thinking you were someone, determined to find out who. She doesn't know that you were wrong. That you are no one. That you failed. The city waits with its mouth rusted open for prey just like you, and when enough of you wander in, those jaws snap shut. Losing your arm was merely an alteration of your outward appearance to match its contents. Unfinished. Incomplete. Lacking purpose.

Clara doesn't know all that, and thus doesn't know how deep and wide her words cut into you. You storm out of the room in a huff, not caring about games or flowers or anything else. Your eyes are hot with tears and your nose leaks. You aren't even exceptional in your failure.

You find a small washroom and sit on the necessary, holding the door shut since you can't find a lock or catch on the door. Little shreds of light appear where the door doesn't fit its frame. You stare at them for what could be hours, or days, tracing them with your eyes over and over.

When you emerge, you feel driven to apologize to Clara, and retrace your path to that room, but find it empty, its furnishings destroyed. Cabinets are pulled out, and thick puddles of spilled food and beer seeps into the rug. Cups and empty beer pots are everywhere. The very walls of this room seem to droop, blackened by smoke, and a jagged burn halo stretches wide across the floor.

Blood. So much blood. Beatrice's flower garland hangs from the mirror's gilt-frame.

You must find that hallway again. The one with the windows overlooking the property. You must get out.

The old woman walks the halls of this immense, sepulchral house. Noises of carousing and merriment echo throughout, with occasional screams and stretches of ominous silence. Her skirts jingle, heavy with coins.

It is in one of those silent moments that she sees the relieved outline of a door under the dirty wallpaper. She tries the tarnished brass knob, but the door is locked.

"Of course it is," she mutters to herself. "Of course."

With a sigh and some muttering, the old woman feels around on the door until she grazes the edges of a small keyhole. Crouching down, she grabs her right forefinger in her fist and peels the skin down until it bunches at her knuckle, exposing clean white bone. She shoves her finger in the keyhole and unlocks the door, pulling the skin back up as she steps into an old-fashioned study.

Unlike the other rooms in Drogado's house, this one is tidy. The hardwood floor has been cleaned and swept, the matching beige sofa and armchairs are old but cared for, and the piano gleams like a shock of black ivory. Even the bookshelves have been dusted. Candles burn in two tall, silver candelabras, which the old woman considers an oversight; technically, the room is unoccupied.

A body, newly dead, occupies one of the armchairs. She wears a blue dress that would have looked elegant on someone with narrower shoulders. Her face is flushed, and the blood vessels in her neck are swollen. The skin around her eyes, nose, and fingertips is a soft, grayish blue, and her mouth hangs open, exposing crooked, yellow teeth.

"Poor girl," the old woman says, clucking her tongue. "Heart attacks are for fat old men, dear."

Leaving her for the moment, the old woman examines the bookshelves, finding that they are filled with mounted photographs arranged like books. She pulls one out, smoothing its edges with her thumb only to watch them curl back up. The photograph

shows a young aristocrat whom she recognizes as
Count Drogado.

"How long ago was this taken?" she asks herself. "And how
many times since have you passed out naked in the library?"

Drogado was thin and handsome then, standing in a line
with a handful of now-forgotten heads of state holding
flutes of champagne. Their suits are sharp, tailored in
the old style, and ornamented with epaulets and military
insignia. A caption is written on the mounting board in
pencil: *Count Drogado and etc.*

She examines more pictures and finds them to be much
the same: Drogado talking with presidents and titans
of industry, clasping hands with champion athletes,
caught mid-waltz with radiant young women. Crowds
of people clutter the backgrounds of these photos,
which were clearly taken indoors, possibly even in this
house. Liquor is present in nearly every photograph,
and wisps of smoke obscure the clarity of the images
here and there. She remembers these men and women,
and the coins they carried. Most of the photos are
captioned in pencil, but none of their subjects are
identified apart from Count Drogado.

Gradually, as the old woman makes her way around the
bookshelves, the photos change. Drogado ages and bloats,
and the timbre of his company grows wilder and more
desperate, and younger. In one such photograph,

he smiles alongside four savage-faced young men as they gather around a fifth who has passed out in an armchair.

"I've seen that suit before," the old woman says, tapping the photograph. "Someone else was wearing it. How many others have died in that suit?"

In another photograph, Drogado—clearly inebriated— kisses the cheek of a young girl. He holds her chin, his fingers bent and his thumb pressing under her bottom lip. Her eyes broadcast fright. Smoke trails up from behind them, its source unseen.

In the final bookshelf, the photos of Drogado capture his current appearance, a mean-spirited caricature of his youth. His face is blotched and rubbery, his body swollen inside his tailored clothes. That once-impish grin has warped into a cruel, imperious sneer.

His companions, meanwhile, are bearded and disheveled transients who seem only distantly aware of his presence, much less the camera's. Their ill-fitting clothes, though fancy, cannot hide bruises and open sores, nor the vacant stares on their bestial faces.

The old woman steps away from the bookshelves and sees a boxy black camera hanging from a coat rack near the door. She picks it up, hefts its weight. Its leather strap is cracked with age, and it rattles when moved.

The old woman puts the camera back on its hook just as the overhead gaslights click off. She turns to the dead woman in the chair, collects her coin, and leaves.

Sweat pours from your body as Count Drogado's hand squeezes your throat. His ring digs into you. At least ten other people stagger in the hallway behind him.

"There he is!" Drogado yells, and gives up a loud "Huzzah!" that his compatriots echo in full voice. They are all inebriated on more than just liquor, looking outright spectral in their slipshod cocktail attire. A few have masques on their ashen faces.

You had been looking for a window, a dumbwaiter, a laundry chute, any means of escape. Meanwhile, a fit had taken this house and sent battalions of mad roisterers out into the halls, mocking the finery in which they were dressed, ripping their shirts open to reveal rashes and oozing sores. There was no escape from them.

Around one corner, you found women with their skirts pulled up and their legs hooked over the shoulders of men with their trousers bunched around their knees. Around another, a group of drunks firing pistols into gaslights for fun. You thought you'd found refuge in a stairwell, only to stumble into a pack of those blue-jacketed chaperons laying into a wailing drunkard with fists and feet, and threatening you with the same.

You ran from them, grabbed the frayed edge of a tapestry, and then it was darkness until you came to in the Count's grip. Now he hands you a masque and pushes you into the motley group gathered around him, and you all follow him one at a time up a gnashing staircase. The woman in front of you is wearing a dress that keeps riding up, giving you a bawdy view that you can't appreciate. You feel sick. All you can do is readjust your masque and try to keep up with everyone else.

A door at the top of the stairs opens into a cavernous ballroom, with mirrored walls and a huge crystal chandelier hanging above the hardwood dance floor. A few of the mirrors are cracked, and some of the light fixtures are broken. What little light remains is uneven and dim.

Musicians are playing on a bandstand at one corner of the room, but they look and sound about ready for corpse blankets. They droop over their instruments, unable to play or even find the correct notes, their efforts reduced to a stridulous racket of grinding strings and sharp, tuneless bleating from the woodwinds. There is nothing human in their eyes.

The Count grabs a candle and pulls out his thick billfold, peeling bills from it. "Has anyone here ever burned money?" he asks the crowd. "Let's burn some money!" He lights some of the bills on fire and tosses them into the center of the dance floor. As the other guests produce matches, the Count passes out money that, article by article, is set alight and thrown onto a small pile that threatens to spread around to the tablecloths and napkins.

"Come on then, Mr. Carey!" Drogado yells, shoving a wad of bills into your hand. You light them on fire and threw them into the pile without fanfare, then wince as the cellist's bow scrapes across the strings.

Drogado holds a paper noisemaker in his mouth, and honks it with gusto as he keeps passing money out to be burned. Soon other guests find a box of them, and some New Year's crackers as well, and fill this dim room with noise while enough money to feed a working-class family for a year smolders in the center of it.

You grab a noisemaker and honk as you join the others in smashing glasses and champagne bottles on the floor. At first, you're only keeping up appearances until you find some means of escape. But breaking things feels good, doesn't it? How long has it been since you felt good? Have your body and mind ever harmonized? Ever since you lost your arm, they've been a cacophony.

A fire starts in the center of the room and some of the guests improvise a dance around it, stripping off their clothing. Drogado conducts them as he feeds the fire with money. The fire accentuates every pockmark and hollow in his patrician face. His nose runs. He is alight with a fanatical glow.

"Sometimes you have to let a party change winds in the moment," he yells at you. "Do you understand? Can you hear what I'm saying!" He throws a powder into the fire that turns the taller flames green, prompting loud whoops from the orgy developing around them.

You grew up in a Scriptural house. You wore plain clothes and washed your face in cold water and ate heavy potluck suppers in the church courtyard once a week, which was also the only time you saw anyone besides your own family. Your family's birth and death dates, and other such registries, are kept in an unmarked book on your father's bedside table. His favorite piece of Scripture is *"be sober-minded; be watchful. Your adversary the devil prowls around like a roaring lion, seeking someone to devour."*

It would be a lie to say that you didn't allow your trousers to be pulled down, your under-breeches torn away and cast into the fire, that you didn't allow yourself the full hospitality of the house. Hands and mouths travel your body like insects swarming meat. And still, you turn your shoulder stump away toward the ground. Your head swims, flails, drowns.

You bridle from several embraces as a trapdoor opens in your stomach and you vomit into a puddle of champagne. Seeing yourself in the mirror, naked and pink, the reflections of Alice, Beatrice, and Clara smile behind you. Alice is holding that bong they share and wearing a baggy morning-coat over her shoulders. Her hand is wrapped in a cloth bandage, and her white dress is spattered red. Blood trickles from between her teeth. From all of their teeth.

The mirror cracks and you turn around. They are standing there as the fire licks higher behind them. Alice holds a chef's knife. She lunges at you and you dodge her by falling.

You crawl, then run from the ballroom, back down those deformed stairs, searching for egress until your bones throb and stiffen in their moorings. Whenever you hear *here comes a candle to light you to bed/here comes a chopper to chop off your head,* your throat goes dry and your pulse thunders in your ears.

The old woman's footsteps echo through the large, empty parlor where her bicycle is parked. Compared to the rest of the house, this parlor is eerily silent, and in far more obvious ruin. The curtains hang in tatters, the ceiling and walls peel away. Insects scurry around under her feet, running from piles of molding food to safety in the wainscoting. As she walks, the old woman kicks trash without meaning to; the floor bears a thick carpet of glass, old clothes, cans, bottles, and other refuse.

"They should let me have a cat," she says to herself. "It wouldn't have to be real. They could spin it from the howling voids at each corner of time if they wanted. Just give me a cat, or something."

Other rooms in this wing of the house are in similar shape, including an old kitchen in worse condition than the one she'd seen previously. The interior had been stained brown by ungoverned dirt and grease build-up, and three of the four stoves' burners had been left on. The old woman had tried to turn them off, but their controls were stuck, and she didn't have time to clean them. How many more kitchens were there, she'd thought, and what shape were they in?

The parlor she currently stands in had once been grand, to judge from the width and ceiling height. Other parts of this dizzying mansion had been neglected, and even defiled, but this section of the house has been abandoned. The old woman had gone down several flights of stairs to access it, and is now far from the party that occupies the ground and upper floors.

A most vile and intemperate party, by her reckoning, that never seems to end.

Someone else must have gone wandering down here too, because she is here to collect a coin, and it seems unlikely that its bearer would have been sent this way purposely. She leaves the parlor through a servant's

exit that leads into a narrow hallway, which ends in
a collapse. In the buzzing electrical light from above,
she can read the profanity scrawled on the walls in big,
loopy writing.

The old woman rolls her eyes, then rolls up the sleeves
of her dress and starts pulling rubble out and tossing it
behind her. The walls tremble. Dust spills down, and as
she makes progress, so does more of the ceiling. It is in
this cave-in that she finds the crushed body of a young
woman in an off-the-shoulder white dress. Her right hand
and forearm are spotted with burn scarring and pearls of
wax; the old woman suspects that she was exploring by
candlelight. She might have been pretty, before all this.

The state of this poor woman's head makes finding her
coin a little tricky, but soon it is in the old woman's skirts
with the others. Afterward, she absently draws a cat on
the wall with her fingernail, tracing its shape over and
over again before walking her bicycle up the stairs.

At the top of a carpeted staircase, you open a door only to
find a brick wall behind it. Those women are singing. You
can hear them. Their voices are as boundless as the wind.

You imagine a gray, dust-swept Heaven where angels
bend themselves over adding machines to calculate the

folly of a life such as yours. Your life as you knew it then, your lonely life, balled up and tossed into the hearth.

You kick the wall, slap your palms on it, yelling that you are trapped. No one answers your cries. You doubt they were even heard. The others, prisoners themselves, are too busy tearing into the Count's endless reserves of contraband.

You walk back down the stairs as singing fills more of the air around you. You enter a hallway with black walls covered by thick red draperies accented with gold stitching. You try a door that was locked earlier, hoping for a miracle. You should know better than to hope.

Steeling yourself as your body goes dark with pain and fatigue, you summon enough gumption to take a run at the door and put your shoulder stump to it. Seven times, you do this. Seven times, the door resists. Your shoulder hurts so much you almost can't feel it. An eighth time and it starts to give. You throw yourself at the door, not bothering to brace for impact, hoping that sheer physics will be enough.

Your eleventh try at the door knocks it loose from its hinges. You kick it the rest of the way and fall into a somber parlor, its walls the color of dark walnut. Two helix pillars twist up between floor and ceiling, and tall, narrow windows allow some light to spill onto the floor. The glass panes are patterned with strange geometrical shapes. They won't open.

A suit of clothes has been tossed over the back of a threadbare divan towards the back of the room, and you put it on. You have to roll up the trouser legs.

Footsteps and voices travel up the hallway outside, and without considering the matter further, you hurl yourself through one of the windows, rolling through the fall as best you can.

Jumping is the hard part. Falling is easy. When you fall, you are a note held by a skilled musician, beautiful for a rare and fleeting moment.

You land hard, trying to spread the impact across your back and shoulders. You shrivel into a fetal position, coughing and trying not to choke on the blood filling your mouth. It hurts to breathe. The land here isn't altogether different from where you grew up. A brick wall in the distance cuts off your view, but you can smell rain and loose earth and skunk, which you've never disliked. These are pleasant contrasts to the stink of stale marijuana smoke and liquor and sweat and death, all emanating from you now.

Somehow, you are walking. The ground is one huge snarl of weeds that hides shallow divots and rocks. Every breath starts a fire in your lungs and yet you gulp down air, damning the pain it causes you.

Every few steps, you look up at the walls of this house, which wax and wane with no regular pattern. The dark bricks pull in any sunlight that hits them, and let none escape. It is a vast, menacing fortress that cuts a jagged line against the soft clouds overhead. The weather is mild and you make sure to step into every shard of sunlight you find on the ground.

At last, a door appears at ground level, set into the rear wall of what looks like a large shed connected to the house. You almost fall upon it. Not knowing how much time you have left until someone from the Count's entourage navigates the house's confusing network of stairwells and finds you, you open it.

You see the black steamcoach from the night you were abducted. Blood surges into your fist. You look around the shed, seeing nothing but cinder block-and-board shelves full of dirty steamcoach parts and greasy rags.

Looking under the coach, you find a rusty wrench and smash open one of the cabin windows with it. You and the man sleeping inside are both startled. He was stretched across the cabin's velvet-cushioned bench, and you find him in a disheveled state. His shirt is unevenly buttoned and untucked, his trousers are backwards, and his collar is smeared red. He is but half your height, with uneven side whiskers.

"Get me out of here," you say.

"Who are you?" he asks. "You're not supposed to be here." He shoves the door open and knocks you back onto the shed's loose gravel floor.

"Help me," you say. "Please. I need to leave." You stand up, clutching the wrench tight in your only hand.

"You're not allowed in here," he says. "You're not allowed outside, there's no way they'd let you outside. How did you get out?"

"Help me." You squeeze the wrench. It, like you, is an instrument of abject, flailing stupidity in the control of something malicious, malevolent, and larger than itself. If it had eyes, it too would mistake the howling, empty void all around it for the presence of a god.

"If they find us in here, they'll kill us both. Get back inside, now." He tries to close the door, but you spring into the cabin and crush his nose with the wrench. He screams. You swell with bitter triumph as you swing the wrench again, and again.

You think about what your parents' faces might have looked like when they found your empty bed. Like his, probably. He begs you to stop and you almost don't. You drop the wrench and collapse against the cabin door. It takes the man several minutes to stir. He's bleeding.

"I'm a prisoner here, too," he says. "They're insane, all of them. The Count and his brides."

"His brides?" you ask. A knot pulls taut in your stomach.

The man crawls out of the cabin and pulls a rope that lifts the shed's door. You step out with him to see the front of the house. The shed sits on a lake of gravel, and a path of that same gravel winds around to the front of the house, which looks more like a derelict castle than a manor. The cracked battlements have been worn by time and weather.

You can see the house's front door, studded with thick iron nails for some reason, and beyond that, the greater measure of the Count's property, overgrown with weeds. A few lanterns hang, unlit, on tall poles arranged in parallel rows, forming a crude sort of arcade down the length of the property.

The man crawls up into his box seat at the front of the coach and tells you to do the same.

"Where are we going?" he asks.

"Away from here," you say. "A train station, if possible."

He starts the coach and you almost weep as it rolls down a wide dirt path to the main gate of the property, then onto a semi-paved road.

Drogado's coin sleeve is empty. The old woman knows which one is his, having memorized the coin catalog long ago, and looks up the production number in her directory.

His coin—a gold bullion—was a new minting, not a reissue or carryover. The dings and tarnishings began early with the death of his father and his inheritance of the family fortune, the lavish parties, flirtations with the occult. Debt. Refusing to pay for work completed on his current estate, purchased to make a permanent home for his bad habits. Borrowing money to entertain increasingly motley collections of guests. Intimidating creditors. Self abuse. Lies. Murder. Perversion of every shape and description.

The old woman has seen old coins that had passed through multiple bearers, the worst of whom could turn a shiny coin black and dull with corruption over the span of one lifetime. She has held them in her hands, turned them over in her fingers, then sent them down the chute to the smelting chamber to be destroyed. Drogado's coin, if it were present, might very well have been ground into dust and blown away.

As the coach picks up speed, its massive engine belching steam everywhere and squealing loud enough to wake the dead, the rough roads bounce you all over your seat.

"Those women," you ask. "You said they're the Count's brides, yes?"

"Yes," is his reply.

"All three of them?" You have to repeat this question as a coal truck, shrouded by dust, returns from the refinery. Even empty, they're loud enough to drown out any voice that isn't shouting.

"Yes," the driver says, nodding. "No priest would perform the ceremony. They all drew their shutters in his face."

"How do you know?" you ask.

"Because I had to stand watch over 'em when the Count and that fat little minister did their come-to-darkness business."

Brown rabbits scatter out of the road as the coach tears past them.

"I only saw a bit of it. They cut a huge circle in the floor in Drogado's study, and a star inside that, and they had this stunning prize of a woman naked and bending over so they could use her like an altar." He cups a hand in front of his chest to demonstrate just how stunning she was.

"They didn't," you say. He has to be lying.

"They did," he says, "I saw it." His face seems sure enough of it. "I didn't see much else before they told me to go look after the brides, so I did. We played pinochle and feather and charades and blind man's bluff for hours, and that's where they got me. I must have blundered around that room for half an hour before I pulled off the blindfold and they were gone."

He pauses to spit.

"Turns out they'd made a rope from some old curtain cords that was long enough to escape from the window. I followed their footprints to the door and the minister's steamcarriage was gone, and the human altar girl was sprawled across the front steps." The driver sniffs, not out of sadness but to pull blood back into his nose. That was your fault. He spits again. "Her neck was broken."

You search his face for some evidence of invention, but there is none.

Five miles out from the house, the driver jerks the coach sharply to the right, running you off the road and into the gravel bed lining it. You almost tumble out of the seat, but before you can ask what the hell he's doing, a white steamcoach rams into you from the left. A glancing blow thanks to the driver's maneuvering, but still enough to wreck the door and almost unseat you again.

As your coach lurches back onto the road, you hoist yourself up enough to see the other steamcoach behind you. Its windows are tinted and it has been fitted with steel siding and thick tyres, but no other embellishments. It keeps pace with your coach until it can swing back to your left and merge into you again, trying to tip your coach off the shoulder.

"What the hell is going on?" you yell at the driver, who ignores you. He keeps your place on the road, barely, but the other coach won't let up. Your ribs grind together every time the coach jolts from impact with your pursuers.

Your driver makes another abrupt turn, this time off the road, barreling over the raw landscape with the other coach right on your heels. As you head straight for a grove of trees, you yell at the driver again, begging him to stop this madness. Each word from your mouth sends a bolt of pain through your body. Branches scratch the sides of the coach. A collision is imminent.

This is where it ends, you think. You spend what you think are your final moments guessing which tree will do what penury and the surgeon's bonesaw could not.

Your father once told a story about when he was a soldier under enemy fire in an abandoned farmhouse. One of the other soldiers kept saying "here it comes" every time the house shook and sagged. Dust and wood chips rained down from above, as your father told it, and cracked support beams groaned in their fittings. *Here it comes,* his compatriot would say, as homemade shells landed closer to their position. *Here it comes,* as the disembodied wall they were hiding behind fell away pieces at a time. *Here it comes,* as they wondered how dying would feel.

"Here it comes," you say aloud.

Your driver waits until the other coach commits to following you before throwing your coach into a tight U-turn that puts it up on two wheels. As you hear the other car smash head-on into a tree, your coach tips over onto its side. When you land, you spit bright red blood into the grass. It won't stop coming.

You crawl away from the coach and see the driver, who hasn't taken the spill much better than you. A rotary pistol hangs from a torn leather holster strapped under the box seat. You take it, wondering why the driver didn't go for it when you stormed in on him in the shed.

The driver sees you advancing on the other coach, which crashed into a thick, gnarled tree that has fallen through its roof. No one stirs or makes a sound within as you approach.

"Give me the gun," the driver says. His voice is strangled, his face braided with agony. The dull red bloodstains soaking through his shirt are evidence of internal rupturing.

"Get back in the coach," you say.

"Don't do this," he says. "You don't know what you're—"

"Get back in the goddamn coach." You turn the gun on him, almost falling from the effort. He backs away.

Seeing that the passenger's side window is still intact, you fire the rotary pistol's entire magazine into it, clenching the trigger until the weapon is exhausted. The window shatters. You look inside the coach and see two men in blue jackets, slumped motionless against the dashboard. One of them has a flower garland around his neck.

You hear a coal truck in the distance as you drop the pistol and return to the coach. The driver leans against it, trying to light a cigarette. Birds chirp overhead.

"Will this thing still run?" you ask him.

"I don't know," he says.

Somehow, though your bodies are broken, you both upright the car. You crawl into the cabin, blood still oozing into your mouth from any number of injuries, and lie on your side while the driver fusses over the coach's battered engine. It fails three times. When you hear it start up on the fourth attempt, you press your face into the cushions.

You have returned to the city.

Drogado's coachman put some coins into your trembling, dirty hand, but not enough for a train ticket. You made up the difference by plucking coins from gutters and steam vents around the train station. A transit policeman wrapped you on the knuckles with his truncheon and told you to move along. You limp away, walking a lap around the train station and returning from the other side, then walking in.

You jumped when your bare feet met the station's cold marble floor, and made a chirping sound that drew some stares and stifled giggles your way. When you bought your ticket, the clerk's eyes fell to the blood caked around your fingernails.

When your train was called, you followed other passengers to the outdoor platform. The oncoming train had three lamps on its front end, arranged like Beatrice's eyes. You crushed your ticket in a fist.

The train home was not crowded, and much of that trip is a blur. You were placed in an aisle seat two rows back from a fetching young woman with long blond hair wrapped in a bun on the back of her head. You disembarked before she did and cannot picture her face at all. Not at all.

Now here you are, scrounging again. A large stone fountain sits outside the city's train station, and you plunge your hand into its foul water for coins, finding cigarette butts and clumps of hair. The transit policeman here is staring at you, but does not approach. You find enough money in the fountain for the omnibus, and wait at the closest stop with a motley assortment of laborers and lower-end businessmen.

Standing there, your body weak and tender, you feel every inch of soil your father tilled, every pound of butter your mother churned, every drop of sweat they ever shed in their lives. The weight gathers around the slimy coins in your pocket.

The first omnibus to arrive turns you away. So does the second. You acknowledge the drivers' reprimands with vacant stares. Your brain is a restless tide bashing at the shoreline of your skull. By the time a cart drawn by a clockwork horse arrives, you are the only one waiting for it. The driver waves you on without looking at you, although his nose wrinkles as you drop your fare in the bucket.

These carts are the poor man's omnibus. They are slower and travel on the city's old trolley rails, so their coverage of the city is less complete.

You almost burrow into your seat, and the other passengers give you a wide berth. Their voices collide in your head as they discuss recent labor unrest and minor personal scandals involving people you do not know. Your focus on the skyline does not yield. You pull your knees up and rest your dirty feet on the neighboring seat, reassuring yourself that the familiar scenery passing by the window is not another illusion.

Every bump and pit in the road reminds your body that it hurts. You squirm as your inner workings dislodge and shift. After a while, comfort is impossible.

This cart is traveling the westbound line, and you disembark at the end. Before your abduction, you kept an illegal residence in an abandoned house in the western quarter of the city, which has burned down to the skeleton in your absence. So have most of the other houses in that row. Red rope has been tied around the site, and wooden signs reading KEEP AWAY and NO TRESPASSING and CAUTION: FIRE DAMAGE hang from it. The fire left sections of brick and a few blackened wood beams behind, as well as a collapsed roof that bubbled up in the intense heat. It looks like petrified smoke.

A policeman sees you wandering around and chases you away. The air is still thick from the fire for about a mile or so, after which it thins out as you turn down a street of quiet, unlit houses. Many of them are rundown and resemble the sort of company house owned by a mill or factory and rented to its employees. Others like you—squatters and vagrants—spoke of them fondly, and some had even lived in them at one time.

You stop in front of one such house, examining the drooping front porch and peeling paint, and remember one man you lived with telling you that his company house needed a lot of repairs due to water damage in the foundation. The company's response was firing him, evicting his family, and replacing them with others too timid to complain.

A light flickers on in an upstairs window and you keep going. The pavement is cool against your bare feet, but it will rub them raw if you don't find somewhere to sleep. Being in the city again still feels unreal. You keep expecting all of it to disappear, to be pulled aside like a curtain by one of Drogado's brides, or even the Count himself, revealing you to be in yet another candlelit room full of doomed revelers and freaks. Your bones ache and rattle in their moorings. They cannot endure more violence.

The sun is halfway set when you see the unsteady glow of an oil barrel fire. You limp toward it to find five people warming themselves around just such a fire, set in a vacant lot overgrown with soft, curly grass. Tall, nondescript buildings, probably warehouses, loom over the lot from three of its four sides. This is probably how that house burnt down, you think to yourself as you approach the fire. You smell liquor in the air, and take that as an explanation for why your presence is unchallenged.

You allow yourself some warmth, then lie down in the grass and stare up at what you can see of the sky. It will be cold soon. Your clothes, which you feel on your body for the first time since your escape from the Count's strange house, will not offer much protection from that, even though the trouser legs have unrolled and cover your feet. The jacket's sleeve swallows your remaining hand. The fabric grinds against your skin and you picture it filing you down to the bones as you fall asleep.

Perhaps that is how your mother and father felt, growing old in that empty farmhouse.

You wake up the first time because one of the people by the fire is searching you for anything valuable. Your response is swift and violent, and you fall back asleep with someone else's blood spattered across your knuckles. That was stupid. They could have regrouped and killed you.

You wake up the second time because a doughy man in blue denim coveralls is nudging your sore ribs with his work brogans. "You better leave," he says, "before I get the foreman to kick you to death." Dawn is breaking, and dozens of men dressed just like him are trudging into work in the warehouses.

Too groggy to argue, you stumble away. Turning onto a side street, you walk through a neighborhood lined by brownstone tenements on both sides. Paper trash blows across the pavement. The sidewalks are empty, save a couple of older women carrying brown paper bags up the steps from little basement shops.

Further up the street, a flower-seller pushes a cart full of potted plants and bouquets, hawking them in a firebell voice to the open windows above. When someone decides to buy something, he puts their selection in a basket on a retractable stick and lifts it up to them. You lean against a wall and watch him repeat this process two, three times. Drogado and his brides seem further away.

You keep walking until you find a short row of boarded-up houses, and smash through the cheap flatwood nailed across the front doorway. That is the last thing you do before curling up on the floor and sleeping.

As the trees thicken into forests, a sudden cloudburst sends rain smacking down all around the old woman. She thinks she can out-pedal the storm and picks up speed. Gritty water soaks through her dress and apron and she bears left on a curve so sharp it threatens to tip her off the bicycle.

She sees muddy tyre treads, the kind left by a steamcoach, and follows them through a rush of unwelcoming trees. Her hair, once immaculate, now weeps down her forehead, undone by the weather.

"I just had to leave my umbrella at home, didn't I," she says to herself. "I saw it right there leaning in the corner. I could have just grabbed it." She slicks her hair back and skids to a halt beside a white steamcoach that had crashed headlong into a tree. Spitting rainwater into the grass, she knocks on the tree, feeling the texture of the bark under her bony knuckles.

The snout of the coach has bent around the tree, and the old woman smells bullet holes before she sees them. Rainwater collects in the exposed engine, now broken and useless. There are two bodies inside the car. Male bodies in blue jackets. The woman pulls a hexagonal coin from behind each man's right ear.

"I'm sorry you had to wait," she says. She spits out more rainwater and remounts her bicycle. As she pedals away, she hears thunder.

INTERLUDE I

———

THE PUDDLE

essica Reeder catches her reflection in a puddle. She would have stepped over or around it without a second thought, but the street is alive with steamcoaches and noise, and thus difficult to cross without waiting. As she steps back onto the sidewalk to wait for an opening, she indulges the vanity of looking at herself.

She is her mother's ghost, right down to the thick shoulders and shapeless waist, the upturned nose that classmates once compared to a pig's snout. Around her, other pedestrians complain about the rainy weather and lament seasonal changes toward less sunlight and harsher wind. They are all, including Miss Reeder, dressed in darker clothing to trap heat.

Miss Reeder steps back from the puddle just before a steamcoach's tyres splash water all over where she'd been standing. Two more pass through before Miss Reeder sees something twinkling in the puddle. She isn't sure how—the sky is ashen after that morning's rain—but it is small, and glints as though light from the absent sun were bouncing from it.

Waiting until an older couple moves out of her way, Miss Reeder crouches down to get a closer look at it, whatever it is. She tries to restrict herself to side-eye glances at her own face, aware that people on the street are giving her strange looks.

When she reaches into the puddle for the object, something grabs her hand. She yelps and tries to pull away, but the phantom grip is too strong, and slides from her hand to her wrist.

"Something's got my arm," she says. She repeats herself until a small group gathers around her. They are well-dressed, probably on their way to the theatre district for a show, not offering to help.

"Is this a trick?" a lady asks. "If you're just going to beg for money, this is an awfully tasteless display."

"No!" Miss Reeder says, annoyed. "Something's got my hand. What is it? Can someone come look?" Again, she tries to pull away. Again, she fails. Something about the grip is familiar. She looks down the street and sees more coaches coming.

"I'm not putting my hands in dirty water," the lady mutters, and others nod in agreement. "Shouldn't have stuck your hands in a puddle in the first place," an older man says.

Miss Reeder would answer that, but yelps instead as she is yanked shoulder-deep into the puddle. One of the bigger fellows watching her steps forward and grabs her free arm, making sure to plant his feet before pulling.

An arm rises from the puddle, its hand gripping Miss Reeder's wrist. It is an exact duplicate of Miss Reeder's arm; the same pigmentation, size, length, even the same dark jacket sleeve. More people gather around as a shoulder, a face, a head break the puddle's surface. With further effort, a full person climbs up from the puddle and collapses into Miss Reeder's arms, knocking her into the street.

Miss Reeder hears screams from the sidewalk, and feels like screaming herself. Any other reactions from onlookers are drowned out as a coach sounds its steamwhistle at them, its engine grunting. More join in as vehicle traffic slows, and a few drivers yell at her over the din. The woman from the puddle recoils as headlamps shine on them. She looks just like Miss Reeder. An exact duplicate, coughing up lungfuls of dirty water, her clothes and hair dripping.

As Miss Reeder pulls her duplicate self out of the street and onto the sidewalk, the woman falls to her knees and retches.

"I'm sorry," Miss Reeder says, not sure why she is apologizing. "Are you hurt? What's happening?"

She looks up and sees people staring at them. Someone fetches a policeman, who approaches them with a hand on the club holstered at his side.

"Ma'am, I need you and—" His eyes move from Miss Reeder to her soaking-wet double. "I need both of you to step away from the street."

Miss Reeder nods and does as told, pulling her double by the arm along with her. Perhaps this sort of thing is common enough that the police can explain it to her. Behind her, coach traffic lurches back into its normal rhythms.

"Now, what's going on here? What's this about?" The policeman's voice has a scolding tone, as though Miss Reeder were a child. "Did one of the theatres commission you to perform some kind of stunt?" He pauses to snort and spit into an alleyway. "Wouldn't be the first time, but this is in awfully poor taste."

Miss Reeder's double gives him a hateful look, spits out a mouthful of water, then pulls out of Miss Reeder's grip and runs across the street without looking for oncoming traffic. She is almost struck by a coach. The policeman curses, pushes past Miss Reeder, and runs after her double. Trembling and upset, Miss Reeder sulks down the street and stomps in the next puddle she sees. It is an inch deep, if that. She looks into it again and sees the reflection of a dust-colored sky. Nothing else.

Miss Reeder tidies up her small kitchen after breakfast. If she doesn't wash up right afterward, the dishes sit in her sink all day and attract flies.

Behind her, in what passes for her sitting room, work beckons. The desk was her mother's, as are most of her furnishings aside from her bed, her typewriter, and the bound stack of professional correspondence next to it. It all has to be typed up that afternoon and mailed no later than 5pm, and this client is merciless on the subject of timestamps. If the postage on the insulated envelope shows *5:01*, she'd better pray for another $5 to fall out of her stockings, because her pay will be short that amount.

Before she sits down at the typewriter, she splashes some water on her face and watches through her kitchen window as tree branches bend to the wind. The woman she'd pulled from that puddle three days prior seems as distant as a dream, and she is confident that she'd imagined the whole thing. She ignores the occasional crimp in her stomach that warns otherwise.

With the washing up done, Miss Reeder cracks her knuckles and unties the bundle of letters next to her typewriter. She starts from the top, and works through to the middle of the stack before pausing to use the necessary. Afterward, she lingers by the mirror that opens into a medicine cabinet, and sees nothing but the wall behind her, as though she weren't there at all.

Miss Reeder's friend Jane leans her bicycle in the hall and wipes her nose and brow with a handkerchief. She's visiting straight from a ride, and is still wearing her cycling knickerbockers and short jacket, both patterned in a bold yellow-and-black checkerboard that repels the eye from her lean, narrow figure. Her hat, a shapeless brown thing, hangs from the bicycle's handlebars and shows visible salt lines from previous rides.

"I really thought the weather cooling down would make riding easier," she says, taking a few slow breaths. "Fool that I was. I hate sweating in the cold."

"How far did you ride today?" Miss Reeder asks, rubbing her eyes.

"Just to the waterfront and back," Jane says, looking for a place to sit that won't be ruined by sweat. "They were unloading a bunch of tobacco down there today. Made me want cigarettes again."

"Well I don't have any," Miss Reeder says, assembling the tea service.

"Dammit, Jessie," Jane says. "There's all this air in my lungs and none of it tastes like anything." *Jessie* is the closest anyone gets to calling Miss Reeder by a nickname. Her landlady calls her Jessica, and her clients calls her Miss Reeder, as do most other people. The word *Miss* sinks into her like a pushpin.

While Jane waits for tea, she appraises her friend's heavy, black typewriter. It is a solid-looking machine, with metal keys that let out a sharp report when pressed. Jane rather likes the look of it; clean lines with no excess ornamentation, modern and industrial. It looks built for function.

"How's business going?" she asks Miss Reeder, her eyes and hands moving to the pile of handwritten letters next to the typewriter.

"Well enough," Miss Reeder says, yawning. "I'd be doing better if I worked for a firm, but I'm not starving to death."

"How do you even read this writing?" Jane asks, holding a letter so close to her face that the paper brushes her nose. "It looks like the folds in a barber's chair."

"Like most things, it takes practice," Miss Reeder says. "And I have more of that to do yet, so I can't linger over tea for too long." Lavender tea, today. She only has shortbread cookies in the cupboard and doesn't feel like making anything.

As she sets the tea service down on her small, scratched table and pulls two chairs up to it, Jane's eyes wander the sitting room. Most of the furniture—and there isn't much of it—looks inherited, and doesn't suit the room at all. Jessie has done her best to make it presentable, but the divan and cushions are too dainty for a boarding house, and the free-standing cabinet in the kitchenette is too tall.

"Have you been sick?" she asks, as Miss Reeder arranges shortbread fingers on a plate. "You look like watered-down lemonade, and I haven't seen you in ages. I was hoping you'd be healthier." Miss Reeder nearly snaps a cookie in half at her friend's impertinence.

"Sorry to disappoint," Miss Reeder says. She hasn't told Jane about the puddle incident, or her subsequent inability to see herself in mirrors. It's been a week since she has seen herself. A chasmal, empty feeling has been interrupting her sleep. Someone who looks just like her, down to the smallest detail, is wandering the city with no obvious way to find her. Apart from not being proper tea conversation, it isn't something she knew how to talk about, even to Jane.

"I'm sorry," Jane says. "I didn't mean to be rude." She hangs her head a little, looking sheepish until Miss Reeder hands her a cookie as a token of forgiveness. Jane really doesn't mean it, the same way that cats mean no particular offense when they lift their tails in your face.

Despite the awkward start, the two have a pleasant visit, and Jane has a lot of news about the scandalous new plays on stage at the raw edges of the theatre district, and the heightened police presence in response to them. Her description of staged vivisections and hidden pneumatic tubes spraying audiences with gore makes Miss Reeder gag, and Jane's equally vivid account of watching a uniformed officer toss three nude actors down a flight of marble stairs makes her blush. It's as if they're trying out all of her father's complaints about the arts, one by one.

When Jane takes her leave, she clutches Miss Reeder's hand and tells her to be well, and to ask if she needs anything. Miss Reeder nodded. "Before you go," she says, "is anything missing? About me, I mean." She pauses in response to Jane's confusion. "Am I missing anything?"

"Not that I can tell," Jane says. "Besides a good night's sleep, I mean."

Miss Reeder smiles as much as she can, then closes the door and returns to her typing.

Miss Reeder has to run after the postman for half a block to hand off her packets of typed correspondence, sealed in a sugar-colored envelope. She clenches her hands together as she watches him heft its weight.

"What is it?" he asks her.

"Typed letters," she says. "Please take it. I lost track of time and it must be timestamped by 5 o'clock."

The postman checks the time on a copper-plated pocketwatch. Seconds pass in beads of sweat on Miss Reeder's neck. The postman draws his red stamp from his hip, dials it to the correct time, and presses it to the postage on the envelope. He re-holsters his stamp and smooths his mustache away from his mouth with thin, ink-stained fingers.

"Ten cents, then," he says, and she pays him with much gratitude.

"Have you seen a woman around who looks like me?" she asks him as he turns away. He turns back and looks her over, which makes her uncomfortable. She is not someone who likes feeling seen.

"Can't say one way or the other," he says. "You're pretty average as far as looks. Could be hundreds of women in the city who look like you."

Miss Reeder ignores his bad manners. "I mean, just like me. An exact double."

"Sorry," the postman says. "Can't help you." He whistles as he walks away.

There are days when Miss Reeder sits by her window,
feeling nothing except the hole digging itself deeper
and wider in her stomach. Her anxiety sprawls as far
and aimlessly as the city does. What does it mean to
have an exact copy of herself running around the city
unaccounted for, and where is she? How did she manifest
within the puddle? Mounting any kind of search would
be impossible. The city is too big, the terms too bizarre
and unseemly.

On other days, Miss Reeder walks tall down streets
lined by brownstone tenements, stepping over articles
of paper trash on the pavement. She smiles at the older
women carrying brown paper bags up the steps from little
basement shops, knowing that she won't see herself in any
street-level windows.

When you don't like what you are, a reflection withheld
can be a blessing. Until the episode with the puddle, every
window and mirror and flat, glossy surface reminded
her that she is unattractive, just like her dead mother.
A reprieve from that is not without benefit. Over time,
maybe she can forget her face, her mannish shoulders
and arms, the straight lines connecting her ribs to her
hips. The wanderings of her reflection still worry her, the
growing hollow in her spirit still worries her, but having
some sense of anonymity from herself is such a relief.

On her way home, with a ream of correspondence under her arm, Miss Reeder walks under a tenement building whose upper windows are open. Men with cigarettes in their mouths lean out from the ones that aren't stacked with laundry.

"Hey!" one of them calls out. "Didn't I just see you downtown?"

She looks up. He is older, crusty-looking, smoking in his undershirt. Hair has spread across and over his shoulders as a consolation for receding from his head.

"No," she says. "I don't go downtown much."

"Neither do I," he says. "But I saw you there, I'm sure of it. How'd you get back up here so fast?"

"You are mistaken, sir," Miss Reeder says, walking away. A tremor ripples through her body, after which she runs back to the window to ask him exactly where he'd seen her. His window is shut, and she almost scoops a stone up from the street to throw at it.

Her vision goes blurry twice on the walk back to her boarding house, and again while she is typing. She manages to get her packet of typed letters to the postman on time, but she stops on her way back home to lean against a lamp post and rest, suddenly exhausted and short of breath.

It felt like her entire body blinked, and she wakes up startled on the sidewalk, her nose burning from smelling salts.

"There you are," says a man to her left, nodding. He wears a tall hat and a periwinkle opera coat, and there are flecks of white in his beard. He looks very well-to-do, tucking the bottle of smelling salts into his vest pocket. "Are you all right?" he asks, helping her to her feet.

"I think so," Miss Reeder says, swaying as she stands up. "Just felt faint for a moment." She pauses and shudders as one of those clockwork horse carts passes by on the street. She hates the sound of those things.

"You look pale," the man says, "and your hands are awfully cold."

"I'm fine," Miss Reeder says, annoyed at the reproach, and walks home. In her necessary, she washes her hands and does find them pale, in the way that frost thins out as it thaws.

A makeshift outdoor market opens up outside the imposing gates of the public cemetery, where Miss Reeder has spent an hour wandering in no particular direction. The day's workload has been light enough to afford her some extra time that afternoon, and she needs to see something green. Given the time of year, there is more yellow and brown present on the trees than anything else, but she makes do. A shawl keeps the seasonal chill from her neck and ears, and as she walks through the narrow lanes between gravestones, she wraps her hands up in it, too.

There are others out that day, and by the time Miss Reeder leaves the cemetery, enough of them are gathered around the gates that a few fruitsellers have pulled their carts around. An enterprising butcher has joined them, which Miss Reeder thinks is a bit coarse. Strolling through a space where death is given some reverence, only to see a line of skinned rabbits hanging from the bottom of a sign that reads "Fresh Meat," jars her.

Still, she passes right by the produce to examine the butcher's stock. He is built like a cobblestone, revealing a few missing teeth as he smiles and says good evening. He has rabbits, and a few small chickens, and six slabs of red meat packed loosely in ice. She buys a rabbit and a piece of that red meat, and carries them home in a paper bag.

That empty feeling she's been carrying around begins to throb, as if newly awakened.

Miss Reeder has never had a huge appetite for meat, preferring vegetables and sweets, but as she cooks the rabbit—no easy feat in a kitchenette—her mouth actually waters. This has never happened to her before. It is the kind of wanting she's only heard about in old songs and hymns. After dinner, she sleeps uninterrupted for the first time in weeks.

Her visits to the butcher grow more common. There are three within reasonable walking distance of her apartment, and she alternates between them. It seems like the polite thing to do. Even with food, she didn't want to express anything smacking of desperation. She buys rabbit and venison and beef and cubes of salted pork belly, and chicken when none of those are available. With each meal, that emptiness stitches itself shut inside her, only to yawn open wider in the morning.

When she meets up with Jane for a walk around the cemetery—no impromptu outdoor market this time, to Miss Reeder's dismay—the first thing her friend says is, "Have you been well? You look gray." This prompts Miss Reeder to look at her hands and sure enough, her complexion is sallow. Not at first glance; it is subtle, as though a layer of soot is spreading under her skin.

The bell of a distant church tower strikes one-thirty in the morning as Miss Reeder stands over her kitchen sink. She'd eaten half a chicken for dinner that night, but hunger returned earlier than usual. Her pulse quickens as she pulls a cut of raw beef from her icebox and thaws it under some hot water from the sink, preparing to cook it.

She holds it in her hands, watching flecks of ice dissolve in water. Sweat pushes through her thin nightshirt. She wonders if her double self feels this way, alone somewhere in the city, standing over a sink with raw meat in her hands, thoroughly indecent.

She's felt stares, here and there, from strangers: the man at the bank, the postman, a young couple window-shopping in the butcher shop, a one-armed homeless man picking coins out of a gutter. Where had they seen her? What shape was she in?

Even Jane has noticed it. "Those men are staring at you, Jessie," she'd said the other day as they waited for the omnibus. "Do they know you?" The men in question were sitting at an outdoor cafe, drinking red liquor out of small glasses.

"No," Miss Reeder had said. The omnibus had arrived shortly thereafter, stopping with its doors right in front of her, and Jane. Only Jane's reflection had stared back at them from the glass.

"There's an odd trick of the light," Jane had said. "It looks like I'm standing here by myself." She'd laughed as the doors opened and Miss Reeder rushed aboard, knocking a disembarking passenger aside.

Miss Reeder turns off the water and drops the meat in the sink. The emptiness gnaws at her as she wipes her hands on a rag. Her fingers tingle and her vision goes greasy.

When she wakes up on her kitchen floor, she grabs the meat from the sink and eats it raw, shoving it into her mouth with both hands as birds greet the rising sun. She eats too fast to breathe, but her body settles itself after she swallows the last bite.

She waits for a couple of hours before leaving to pick up that day's correspondence, her hands streaked red.

Two weeks pass, during which time Miss Reeder's typing suffers in quality, earning an official reprimand from one of her clients. She reads it once, then discards it. She loses another client altogether, and forces herself to work until sunrise for a few successive days to avoid losing a second. Her fingers stutter on the keys and her eyes burn in their sockets.

While pacing around her apartment to stretch her legs, Miss Reeder hears voices from downstairs. One of them is Jane's, and the high pitch suggests trouble.

Miss Reeder walks downstairs to find her landlady's door cracked open, and Jane standing in front of it. She talks a mile a minute under the scrutiny of the landlady's sharp little eyes, obscured by the chain clutching her door to the wall.

"Jane?" Miss Reeder asks. "Are you all right?"

Jane stops mid-sentence and runs to her friend, grabbing her in a hug that presses her face into the shoulder of Jane's light brown jacket. It is damp and salty-smelling.

"I thought I saw you get pulled into a coach," Jane says, trying not to cry. "I called out for you, could have sworn it was you."

Miss Reeder doesn't care much for hugs, but she lets this one linger, and feels herself tremble in her friend's arms. Her hand is a dead, flat gray against the brown of Jane's jacket.

"Where did you see this?" she asks.

"The theatre district," Jane says, wiping her nose. "I was leaving a lecture at one of the guignol-houses and saw them drag that woman into a coach when I was unlocking my bike."

"Lectures?" Miss Reeder grunts out a weak laugh.

"Yes," Jane says. "It's not always blood and murder, you know. They have lectures as well."

"About blood and murder."

"About lots of things," Jane says. She grabs Miss Reeder's arm. "I'm so glad it wasn't you."

"Did you see who did this?" Miss Reeder asks. "You mentioned a 'they' a second ago."

"No," Jane says. "It was dark. I only know there were three of them."

"Did you tell the police?"

"I wanted to check on you first."

Miss Reeder keeps her relief to herself.

The following evening, Miss Reeder takes the omnibus to the theatre district. It drops her off at the north end, where brightly-lit marquees drown out the gaslamps. Sharp-eyed young boys hawk playbills and programs, belting out the evening's attractions in exuberant voice.

Miss Reeder takes one program as a courtesy (and because the boy stands in her way), and walks south, against much of the foot traffic. Steamcoaches hiss and honk and bottle-neck in the street, keeping her on the sidewalk. She dodges smartly-dressed couples darting past and waves away clouds of cigarette smoke from nervous-looking men pacing in front of the theatres.

An empty feeling expands through her body, spreading to her limbs and making her fingers and toes tingle. Even in the brisk evening air, she begins to sweat.

The marquees dim as she ventures south, and the theatres themselves get smaller. The people carousing at this end of the district are rowdies, chasing perverse entertainments until the raw hours of the night. Most of them are men, and most of them radiate intellectual curiosity, even as they are drawn to salacious performances and lectures about murder, occultism, drug use, moral debasement, and other vulgarities. Every social class is represented among them, in fits and starts, but no matter how well-off or downtrodden, they all look alike: untucked shirt tails, bent and dented hats, jackets glistening with affixed chains and brass rivets.

Most of all, Miss Reeder notices their swollen, pockmarked faces; living at night erodes the complexion. She tries to picture Jane walking unnoticed among them, and could not. Even in her cycling clothes, she would be a candle in the dark among these people.

The corner where her double had been taken is a dark one, with nothing but low light from an adjacent guignol-house to illuminate it. A trash barrel sits on the edge of the curb. It needs emptying.

Miss Reeder looks both ways before stepping into the street, even though vehicle traffic has thinned along with most other signs of civilization down this way. Maybe if she puts herself where her double had been taken, she will stumble across something that would make sense of this whole affair.

All the while, her stomach hurts and her body craves meat. She imagines the smell of blood in the air.

A lady's shoe—black, broken, old—has been left in the street, and she shows it to a spindly-bodied man in a black rivet coat and trousers who smokes in the doorway of the guignol-house.

"Excuse me? Beg your pardon, but do you know who this belonged to?" Miss Reeder asks.

The man looks her up and down before taking the shoe from her. "No one in particular. Whores are always swapping shoes. A lot of them probably wore this one." His mouth threatens a smile. "Is she a friend of yours?"

"No," Miss Reeder says. "She disappeared around here, is all. Stepped into a black steamcoach with three people inside."

"A lot of people step into coaches around here," the man says. He glances at the door as a loud series of gasps sound from inside.

"What's going on in there?" Miss Reeder asks.

"One of the city's doctors is treating us to an edifying medical lecture," the man says.

"That didn't sound very medical," Miss Reeder says.

"It's on the subject of venereal disease," the man says, shrugging in the direction of a poster sitting in the window. "He must have brought out a visual aid." He smirks. His skin glows in the light, but not in a healthy way.

"This woman I spoke of," Miss Reeder says, "she...well, she looks exactly like me." She blushes, and feels dizzy.

"Have you seen a woman who looks just like me around here recently?"

The man's smirk falls into a scowl. "Look, lady, if there's an angle here, I'm not getting it." He flicks his spent cigarette away and hands the shoe back to her. "I'm going back inside. If you want to see the show, you can buy a ticket at the box office. You haven't missed much."

Miss Reeder throws the shoe on the ground as the guignol-house door slams shut. Her walk back to the omnibus stop is arduous; waves of ravenousness tear through her, disturbing her balance and vision. Her mouth goes dry. Sweat drips down her arms and soaks through her clothes and shawl. Vehicle traffic thickens again and the noise bites into her ears.

She pauses to catch her breath, leaning on a fence that covers an alley between two upscale theatres. A fat older man sweeps cigarette butts into the gutter as a hearty, middle-class couple stroll past, their arms linked. Miss Reeder's eyes dart from their pink, healthy flesh to her own, what little she'd exposed of it. It is gray and rough.

Miss Reeder pictures her double lying cold on the side of some dark street. Then she pictures herself following that couple and bashing their heads into the bricks until they split open, and quickly shakes both images from her mind.

An exclamation from up the street catches her attention, and she stumbles over to that very couple, standing with a few others in evening dress and pointing at a spot in the street.

"That coach just ran over a rat, I think!" the lady of the couple says, her vexation obvious. "It didn't even stop."

Miss Reeder looks at the rat as more coaches drive over it. It is a fat one whose head and back have been crushed against the cobblestones. She sees wet blood matting in its fur, and without thinking, she dashes into the street and grabs it. Once she finds a hole big enough to fit her mouth over without difficulty, she drinks the rat's blood, wringing it with her hands like a dishrag.

What drowns out all the honking and screaming is the sound of her heart roaring in her ears as that wound inside her seals itself shut.

Jane dabs a wet washcloth over Jessie's forehead, then pulls her bedsheets up under her chin.

She's been asleep for three days, at least. Her landlady says the police brought her back to the house, disoriented and covered in blood, and that she hasn't left her room since then. *Thank heavens I came calling when I did,* Jane thinks, not for the first time.

Leaving Jessie's bedroom, Jane passes by the typewriter, and the scattered pages of correspondence next to it. She leafs through them, still unable to read any of the sloppy penmanship. She lingers at the typewriter, pressing the 'R' key and watching the letter strike itself onto the page over and over. She stops when she hears Jessie stirring in bed, thinking she is waking up, but her friend has only shifted position. Even in sleep, she looks troubled.

Jane sits down at the edge of the bed and presses one of Jessie's hands between hers. In some ways, she is still sitting there.

PART II

Reality has a way of intruding. Reality eventually intrudes on everything.

—Joe Biden

ou move from abandoned house to abandoned house, keeping to the north end of town where there are fewer development interests. When other derelicts stumble upon a house you've found and take shelter there, you find another. When a tree branch casts the wrong shadow on the floor, you leave. One house which had been painted gray, windows and all, had an attic whose door was bolted shut. You left when scratching noises and low, muttering voices interrupted your sleep.

Every pair of eyes in every face that isn't yours is a threat. For days, weeks, you roam the city with nothing to guide you but half-remembered instinct. After your ordeal, your stomach is an eye that will not open. You fast for weeks, subsisting on dirty water, your head and limbs aching from dehydration.

What little money you scrounge up goes to buy beer and brandy from corner shops. Their storefronts don't even allow enough light to glint off the coins you press into their grubby hands.

One afternoon, you stare at the exposed brick wall of an empty cellar and count the bricks, imagining a rat running through the labyrinth made by the crumbling mortar between them. This is how you justify drinking so much, so often. It blunts all form and shape from your thoughts. It is the pretense of introspection.

You panhandle on the south end, where the people are wealthier, and many are new to the city and unaware that someone asking them for spare coins might not spend them on anything edifying. You wear your clothes from Drogado's mansion down to rags, and rip off the sleeve covering your missing arm when they get too filthy to keep. You travel by clockwork horse carts that need to be wound at each stop, so it takes longer to get from one place to another.

Since they are cheaper than the omnibus, they are more crowded. There is still work to be found in the city; six piano factories, mills and canneries, facilities that make shoes and ready-to-wear clothing. The docks were full of stevedores loading and unloading cargo ships, their hands rough from shaggy ropes and wooden crates. They live in the shadows of those mills and factories, their lives measured in miles of bricks and wide cargo doors and oily pavement, and the occasional blast of steam from vents in the sidewalk.

You remember this life of waiting to be picked for labor, hoping to impress and be given something permanent, knowing that your best would never be good enough. Sooner or later, that idleness would creep in and make you sleep entire days away. It made you slow, easily distracted. Stupid.

The old woman clutches a handful of coins in her veiny hand as the Count, his tuxedo stained and reeking, holds court with a handful of guests who can barely keep their eyes open. He sits in a grand banqueting chair, and his guests sit in smaller matching chairs, all around a table that has been overturned into an ankle-high pile of used plates, cups, food, and other garbage. The table's surface has been burnt with cigarettes, and rude words have been carved into it with a pen-knife.

"My brides each selected an architect to build a portion of the house," he says, "so this place is kind of a vortex." He laughs, almost giggling. "We still can't connect parts of it to electricity or plumbing." He claps one of the guests on the back. "You're a married man, aren't you? You know how this works."

The man groans, his jaw slack.

"You're telling me," Drogado says. "They'll have their way, though, especially my brides. And really, I had this house built for them, so they deserve a say in its construction, you know?"

"Where am I?" a dazed-looking woman asks as she pours warm champagne down her neckline.

"Where are they?" the Count asks, perhaps deliberately misunderstanding her question. "Looking after my guests in some capacity, I'm sure. Entertaining them with a parlor game. I swear, they know thousands of those." He doesn't seem too bothered by their absence, the old woman observes, but emotions are hard to discern with the upper orders. Either that, or he's too drunk to register anything besides dumb confidence.

"The lesson to be learned here," he says, "is that wives don't want what's yours as much as they want new things and then claim to share them with you." He smiles and raises his glass. "Any gentleman sitting here with me will agree."

One of the gentlemen slides off his chair and onto the floor, almost unconscious. Another one belches. The woman who spoke earlier smashes her champagne glass on the floor and sulks in her chair. All the old woman can do is roll her eyes at this scene and take her leave.

As a boy, you accompanied your parents to town for reasons you cannot remember. A homeless woman waylaid your parents on the street and asked them to give her money. Your father removed his coat from his broad shoulders and the woman thanked him as she wrapped herself in it. The wind must have bitten right through your father's sweater as he told passers-by not to help the old woman outside the scrivener's workshop; he'd already given her his coat. The rest was up to God. You and your mother said nothing.

You think of that old woman, and of all the other times you said nothing when something was called for. You wonder if anyone had ever told her that silence was the purest democracy, and if she believed them, or if she was as lonely as you are.

Lonely people live on the periphery. They wake up often in the night due to primitive survival instincts that are muffled in more social people. They die earlier. By all rights, you should be dead already. When you occupy a house, you keep it like a tomb, cold and still.

Your days stretch long with boredom, and your nights fill to overflowing with the sort of wanting you'd heard in the verses of old hymns. In those moonlit shards of time, you think of Alice and Beatrice and Clara, and the ways they looked at and touched and hurt you.

Your ribs are crushed glass in your sternum. A few of
your teeth loosen and fall out. You spit them away. Smoke
flumes through the gaps they leave behind.

Your father and his brothers built the house you grew
up in. It had flaws. Some of the floorboards creaked
and bowed where they didn't meet the struts. The roof
was laid crooked over the kitchen. Two of the windows
slanted to the right. These flaws were accepted, adjusted
for, forgiven. So it is with your body. If you caught fire
right now, you would let yourself burn down to the wick.

For now, anyway. How long until your mind resumes
bashing against the cage of your skull? That man who
left an empty bed in his family's home to squabble in
vacant lots and shipyards for a day's wages, who has
led a wastrel's life, who let himself be pulled into one
debauchery after another as Count Drogado's prisoner—
how much of him can you forgive?

You ladle water from a public birdbath into your dirty
mouth, and look across the street at a policeman directing
steamcoach traffic. A group of men kneel on the sidewalk
outside a seedy shopfront, smoking and playing skully
with bottle caps. A plan cycles through your head to start
a fight among them, attract the officer's attention, steal his
sidearm, and use it on yourself.

You were broken long before you lost your arm.

You have settled into an old carriage house whose top floor has caved in. More abandoned houses crush into it from both sides, and the few inhabited houses in the neighborhood are divided into one-room tenements for people much like yourself.

When you first arrived, the carriage house's floor and walls were quite alive with vermin, and you slept with your hands clamped over your mouth to keep anything from crawling inside. The floor wriggled under you at night, and every morning saw new welts rising like bread from where you'd been bitten. You looked at the dirt-caked walls, soggy in places from where vermin had eaten at them, and gave serious thought to the possibility that you would be eaten alive in your sleep.

Something drew the vermin back, however, and now there are none to be seen. The house is still crumbling away, with huge holes where the steam pipes were torn out and not a single unbroken window to be found, and the kitchen area overtaken by hillocks of rotting garbage, but it is quiet. Weeks pass, and it is left undisturbed by police and other transients. You grow to like how well the sitting room area catches and distributes sunlight, and the general proportions of the house, and the look of the metal staircase spiraling up through the top of the ruined upper floor.

The house opens into a narrow dirt alley, with the backside of an enormous brick warehouse sitting across from it. The two roads perpendicular to the alley are busier, as the people who live there primarily live on the streets. They form tight knots on the sidewalk and pass a cigarette or flask around, they throw dice against the curb, they run to the clockwork horse carts to scrounge and beg for change. More than once, you have walked past a man leaning against a wall or sitting on a stoop, staring vacantly ahead, his eyes soft and unfocused. These people are so ugly, you catch yourself thinking, so mangy and feral and underdeveloped. Can't they see themselves?

Can you? While the neighbors you grew up with toil in fields and drive steamplows and threshers and herd livestock, you sit half-covered in a dirty blanket and stare at the wall. Days pass between your movements. Your stomach slows itself to accommodate your inactivity. It waxes as the muscles in your arms and legs wane. Little by little, the anxiety and pain and fear drain away, replaced by anesthetic stupor. You stop missing your arm. Your wanting ceases. You function as a machine operated by primitive impulses. Thirst. Sleep. Even these are dimmed by the fog rising within you.

How long has it been since you've seen your own face? Reassemble the mirror in your brain. See if the well-scrubbed farm boy you once were stares back at you.

One by one, dead animals appear around the carriage house. Rats at first, some of them plump and bordering on diabetic, then birds, then other rodents. You see new ones every day, soft and limp in the dirt in front of your house. No blood. Never any blood. Their little necks are broken.

It is pleasant, your life, in the same way that decay smells sweet at the edges.

After scavenging enough coins to eat, you return home with fried fish and beer in your belly and a few coins jingling in your ratty pocket. An old woman in a smart gray suit is kneeling in the alley, making no hesitation as you draw near. She turns a dead rabbit over in her gloved hands.

"So many dead animals surrounding this property," she says, her voice unsteady. "Here's another one." She holds up the rabbit, a gray-brown little thing with big hind feet.

You watch her, unsteady on your legs. Your knees ache, and as you shift weight from foot to foot, pain glimmers in your ribs. You're never comfortable, are you?

"How many is this, ten? Twelve?" The woman returns the rabbit's body to the sidewalk. "Too many. It'll escalate to cats and dogs before long." She stands up, wincing as one of her knees pops from the exertion.

You see a white bicycle leaned against the door to the carriage house. It can't belong to anyone else. This neighborhood is all squatters like yourself. None of you could afford a bike, and you're not sure you could ride one. It has to belong to this woman, whoever she is. She looks like someone who would ride a bicycle.

Frowning, you nudge the back tyre with your foot, prompting a startled "hey!" from the old woman. You look down at her on the sidewalk. She has narrow, cold eyes that study you for a moment. You read surprise in her face, and alarm, and disbelief.

"Move your bicycle," you say to her. "It's blocking my door."

She doesn't move. "You can see it?"

"Yes," you say, now puzzled. She's too well-groomed to be the sort of crazy you're used to, and must be some new, high-born variety.

"Don't touch it with your bare hand," she says, hurrying to the bicycle and pulling it away from you. "How are you doing this?"

"Doing what?" you ask.

"Talking to me," she says. "Seeing me. You shouldn't—"
She interrupts herself. "You're killing all these animals,
aren't you." Her eyes narrow and you are suddenly cold.
"These rats and rabbits out here, it's you doing it."

You're affronted by her accusation, and make no secret
of it. "Why would I do that? And how? Last I heard, you
need two hands to catch a rabbit." You point to the empty
air where your arm used to be, the only part of you that
never hurts or wants or complains.

She clearly hadn't noticed your missing arm, and is
properly embarrassed. "Then who is—"

"They're just rats and vermin. Leave it alone."

"Sir, I must insist—" she begins again.

"If it was me down there, would you be here?" you
ask."Kneeling over me, clucking your tongue like my
life mattered?"

"Yes," she says, "because it does."

"No," you respond, "it doesn't. Embrace the end, lady."
Saying it makes you laugh. It's a thought you'd held to
your heart through so many lonely nights, but actually
hearing it from your own mouth, it sounds so juvenile.
And, because you're drunk, it strikes you as funny.

The old woman does not laugh with you. The lines in
her puckered old face are arroyos dug into the palm of
an endless, dusty prairie. The blacks of her eyes are two
blind idiot mouths, screaming forever.

"I don't think that's funny at all," she says. She turns her
back to you and you watch her leave, not stepping into
the house until you are sure she is gone.

A smear of blood across the dirty floor welcomes you, and
it stops at the lifeless, broken body of Count Drogado's
coachman. It takes a moment for you to recognize him,
and another for the implications of this to cut through the
numbness that has filled the vessel of your body.

It all rushes back at once, like a bright lantern flicking
on in the darkness. You turn to run and there they are
in your doorway, all three of Drogado's brides. Alice
and Clara hold suitcases. Beatrice's third eye blooms in
her forehead.

Alice opens her suitcase and a bong rolls out, landing on
the floor with a solid thud. She shakes the suitcase and
a dead rabbit falls at her feet. You kick the dead rabbit
out into the alley as you run, but a hand pulls you back
by what remains of your collar. You thrash and kick at

them, screaming yourself dizzy, at which point Alice slaps you full across the face. You'll never know if you would have returned the blow, because she rips up one of the floorboards and lays into you with it. You crumple to the floor, gasping and wheezing, and two of the three brides fall upon you with punches and kicks. You flail your arm around, trying to create some room for yourself to crawl away, but that only encourages them. Their blows land with increasing force.

You wake up looking straight up at the sky, sooty and gray as dusk approaches. The rough grit of the alley's dirt floor is cool to the touch. Dogs are barking somewhere off in the distance. You roll to your side, finding yourself at eye level with cigarette butts that have been trampled into the dirt. You understand, in a physical way, how they feel.

You crawl out of the alley and onto the blotchy sidewalk. A sickly odor rises up from garbage fermenting in the trash barrels left at intervals along the street. One side of your head is matted down with blood, and your right knee and left hand were badly scraped by your landing. A piece of cellophane flies overhead and you watch the breeze toss it down the street as you regain your composure.

After pulling yourself upright, you lurch down the street and find a police whistle hanging from its pole. Your lungs ache as you blow into it. Birds scatter from their perch on a nearby awning. Garbage reeks in a nearby alley. You blow a second time, and lean against the pole while you wait, careful not to trample any of the flowers growing around its base.

No police answer the whistle, of course. This city has taught you that, sometimes, no help will come, even if you ask for it. And even if it would, you're not worth it.

Smoke edges out the garbage smell, and you turn to see Clara smoking, alone. She smiles at you, blinks her eyes in succession. The bong's tube has broken, so she holds it shut when she inhales. Little filaments of smoke escape from between her fingers.

Clara beckons to you and you walk with her back to the carriage house. Why? Why are you doing this?

As the other two watch from inside, Clara tends your head wound with a kindness you've never felt in any hospital. Every time she swabs alcohol on your head, or wipes away blood, her bosom brushes against your face. You turn your head out of propriety at first, but eventually you just hold still and let it happen.

"How did you get away from us?" she says, after drawing deep from the bong.

You buckle where you stand. "I jumped out of a window." Clara's fingers run through your hair as you look up at Alice and Beatrice. They both have blood on their hands and dresses. Your blood.

"I won't go back," you tell them. "You can't make me."
Clara presses a finger to your lips and traces your
earlobe with her finger. She sweeps her hair away from
her forehead and two more eyes yawn open, making
four in total.

Run from them. Run, you idiot. Get as far away as
you can.

The brides attack the kitchen, shoveling muck and
garbage out into the tiny square yard behind the carriage
house. Their vigor is inexhaustible. They grunt and sweat,
rolling up their sleeves and skirts, their bare arms thick
with sludge as they hurl bucketfuls of detritus out the
kitchen window. As the floor is exposed, so are bones. You
recognize some of them as rats, raccoons, rabbits. The
brides mount the skull of a large dog above the empty
gap where a stove was once installed; they paint an X
between its empty eye sockets.

Other bones don't belong to any animal you've seen.
They're too long and heavy. Alice snaps one over her leg,
explaining that she wanted to hear what noise it would
make. You stare at her just a moment too long and she
throws one half of it at your head.

You take your leave of the house and take a clockwork horse cart downtown to rummage through what a block of restaurants has thrown away. Everything below your ribs is an inarticulate weight.

Sitting against the brick front of a dry-goods shop prompts a well-dressed woman to drop coins at your feet. You remain there for an hour or so, until a policeman's baton swats you further up the street. It's mostly women out today, and a pattern is soon established; they look at the nub that ends your shoulder, then the cracks in your bare feet. Whether they spare coins for you or not, they all follow this pattern.

An evening chill sends you into beer shops, one after the other, until you find one that will sell to an obvious vagrant like yourself. Then back to the horse-drawn cart and the carriage house. The brides are still within, smoking and combing each others' hair. There are four hands of cards dealt on the floor. Clara's eyes guide you down to play.

The four of you play Crazy Eights, the rules of which are largely a mystery to you. The brides nudge at your shins if you deliberate over your cards for too long.

"How do you all know so many games?" you ask, each word blurry at the edges.

"Picked them up here and there," Beatrice says. "Our parents taught us some. We didn't have much money, so we had to entertain ourselves." She switches the suit to clubs, forcing Alice to draw from the deck.

"Did they teach us this one?" Clara asks. "I can't remember."

"No," Alice says. "They were long gone by the time we started playing cards. Father didn't think that was proper for girls." She snorts as she finds a five of clubs and slaps it on the discard pile. "We're better at it than he ever was."

"He was a gambler, then," you say, to no response except the percolation of the bong as Beatrice lights it. Your gaze sheepishly returns to your cards. Stupid, stupid.

"Do you not like games?" Clara asks you.

"I do," you say, although you aren't sure if that's true. Games with the brides are a tense affair. The stakes are never certain. They shift under your feet. "We just play so many. More than I'm used to. I grew up on a farm and there weren't any other children around."

"Your parents didn't teach you?" Clara asks.

"No," you say, closing the door to that subject behind you.

"All we have is each other," Beatrice says, "and even sisters run out of things to talk about eventually. So we play games to pass the time." She changes the suit to hearts.
"We get bored," Alice says. "So bored."

"Oh, everything bores you," Beatrice says. "Even in Drogado's madhouse, you get bored."

You panic at the mention of Count Drogado's name and focus on the discard pile as much as possible. You let your face go slack, hoping it doesn't betray you.

"I wonder if he misses us yet," Clara says, laying down a queen of hearts.

"I can't imagine he's noticed," Beatrice says. "The way he carries on."

Clara stops and thinks for a moment. "He'll notice that I'm gone, I think." She pauses, card in hand, to toke from the bong.

"But not Alice," Beatrice says, taking the bong back and pulling from it herself.

"I didn't say—"

"Yes you did." Beatrice sets her cards face-down on her thigh. "That's exactly what you said." You attempt to interject, but Beatrice cuts you off. "Alice is right here and she isn't deaf. Don't pile on the insult by calling her stupid."

Alice slaps Clara's cards out of her hand. The three of you watch Clara pick them up, and Beatrice smiles. The game continues, and Alice's helpful nudges become kicks. By the time you fall asleep, your legs are mottled with bruises.

The brides produce dominoes and tell you to join them for one game. This is a lie. You stay up half the night.

As they smoke, they tell you in intervals about the time they wandered down to the edge of the river to watch the gondola singers. Alice explains them as older men who sang for money as they paddled long, narrow boats up and down the canals that passed for streets where they grew up. After each song, the crowd would applaud and toss coins into the singer's boat.

"Clara's favorite was the fat man with the bristly mustache who sang in French," Alice says. They all laugh.

"I was a child," Clara says, "I couldn't even understand the words. He made me laugh. He would waggle his eyebrows and the wattle under his chin and bare arms would shake." She imitates this as best she can, laughing until she coughs and upsets the dominoes.

"Yes, and then when you tried to throw him a coin, it bounced off the tip of the boat and plopped right into the water," Alice says. Clara blushes and slaps her sister's shoulder. Alice responds with a slap that draws blood from Clara's nose. Beatrice laughs until a volley of coughing stops her.

"It's the truth!" she says through mouthfuls of foul smoke. "Clara cried like she'd been stung by a bee."

"She didn't even see him dive into the water," Alice says, resetting the dominoes with her bloody hand. "We had to turn her around so she could see him bob up out of the river with her coin in his hand."

"I don't know how he ever found it," Clara says. "That water was disgusting." She lifts up the hem of her skirt to soak up the blood trickling from her nose. Her other hand finds yours. She asks if you ever saw anything like that as a child.

"Not like that, no," you say, eager to pull your hand away. Beatrice blows a wall of smoke around you, blocking out the other two entirely. It stings your eyes and nostrils.

"It wasn't the same coin," Beatrice whispers, her face solemn. "I had to go find the real one." As the smoke dissipates, she presses a domino into your hand firmly. In the interim, Alice has taken the hem of Clara's skirt, and dabs at her nose with it. She does not look pleased.

That same night, a steamcoach rolls through the alley. It is totally black, with smoked windows and a confined driver's box, identical to the coach that brought you to and from Drogado's mansion.

You think of the driver, rotting down to nothing wherever the brides put him.

The old woman pedals down a busy section of the city. Under the midday sun, the streets swell with vehicles, both steam-powered and horse-drawn, and pedestrians whose movements follow no obvious logic or pattern; they are as likely to clump together in the street for conversation as they were to dash across without looking. The old woman has pulled no shortage of coins from the smashed heads of impulsive jaywalkers.

Today was not such a day, however. All of her city appointments today are indoors—five women in hospital beds, three men alone in cluttered boarding-house rooms, one man who passed away in the necessary, and two women who still smell like opium when she finds them together in an alley.

When her last city coin rests in her skirts with the others, she mounts her bicycle and, instead of moving on, heads for the carriage house. Foot and vehicle traffic thins out, then ceases entirely, until all she has for company are piles of trash and ramshackle houses with overgrown lawns. Many of these houses are vacant, home only to vermin and transients who can't afford lodging, even at the lowest boarding houses. She hasn't taken many coins from this part of the city due to the low population, but she has before, and she has repurposed those coins whenever possible.

The carriage house is cleaner than when she last saw it, even though dead birds and rodents still surround the property. The rest of the neighborhood is quiet, rotting away with what little dignity it has been afforded by time and neglect.

The old woman leans her bicycle on the curb and presses her ear against the carriage house door. She hears muffled chatter, and moves to the window. Drogado's horrible brides are within; they play jacks on the floor and pass

a bong around. A man is curled up against the opposite wall, facing away from them.

"What should we invest the money in, do you think?" Clara asks. "Once we have it."

"Railroads, to start," Beatrice says. "Lots of them. They're already putting tracks down through Coal Country. Oil Country's next, then the Coast." She gets her jacks just before the ball touches the floor, a moment that carries more suspense than the old woman had thought possible.

Alice grabs the ball from her and takes her turn, scowling.

"Do you have a better idea?" Beatrice asks her.

"Yes," Alice says. "Don't invest it in anything. Spend as much as we can. If there's any left when the last of us dies, cash it out and burn it." Her arm snaps out like a frog's tongue to scoop up the jacks.

"Do you really want to be a woman in this world with no money?" Beatrice asks. "Again? I certainly don't." She hands the ball to Clara. "It's not the money itself I want. It's the freedom. Men get that for nothing." She frowns and wipes her nose. "We have to buy it."

Alice shakes her head. "Exactly. And when we die, Drogado's money should die with us. Don't be vain."

The man across from them stirs, exposing a stump of a left shoulder. It *is* him, the old woman thinks to herself. Having satisfied her curiosity, at least for the present, she departs on her bicycle, leaving the women to their game.

"You don't suppose he's stopped," Clara says, referring to their husband. "Now that we're gone, I mean."

"Stopped what? Carousing?" Beatrice laughs. "Not a chance. All we had to do was start that stone downhill, there's no stopping it now. As we speak, he's probably stumbling around naked with a sock over his whore-pipe."

"Ugh," Alice grunts. "The masked highwayman routine. I don't miss that." The other two agree.

"You're right," Clara says, picking up her jacks with a snap of her elbow. "And what a relief! I just hope the end comes soon, is all."

"It can come whenever we want," Alice says. "I could throttle him the next time he passes out. Wouldn't even make any noise."

"Or money," Beatrice says. "We won't get a penny if it looks like foul play." She puts the bong to her lips, then coughs.

"Are you saying I couldn't make it look like an accident?" Alice's fists clench.

"No," Beatrice says. "Clara said that. Apparently your influence on the Count is so weak that he'll throw all his guests out into the street the second you drop out of sight."

"That's not what I—" Clara's attempt to defend herself is cut short by a punch in the face from Alice. Beatrice watches them with obvious amusement.

"Be patient, is all I'm saying." She bounces the ball up and down, no longer interested in the game.

The following afternoon, you spend the last of your coin on drink and decide to stroll one of the city's public cemeteries. As you wait for one of the horse carts, the brides gather at your sides, Alice and Beatrice to the right, Clara to the left. Two of Clara's eyes are closed and hidden under her hair. Beatrice's third eye is obscured by flowers strung around her head.

They hum tunelessly at your sides, making a pretty sound that draws in passers-by. By the time you hear the mechanical snorts of the clockwork horse, no fewer than twelve people are waiting with you.

The way to the cemetery passes through the center of town, a noisy hive of horse-drawn and steam vehicles, their bells and horns sounding at unseen traffic violations. Beatrice is amused by the piles of dung left in the street as the carriages pass through, and nudges her sisters whenever a pedestrian has to step over them. You allow yourself to chuckle whenever a well-dressed fellow gets his trouser hems dirty in the street.

"Feet are so strange, aren't they?" Beatrice asks, as you all watch such a fellow remove his shoe and turn it upside down to dislodge a rock.

"They weren't designed properly," Alice says. "Too vulnerable. You can pull a toe right off with just a little torque." She laughs and traps your ankle between her feet, squeezing hard. Her sharp bones dig into yours.

You wince and the other two giggle silently, even as Clara leans against you. The other passengers glance at you, filing the four of you away as an example of Eccentric City Life, to be shared with straight-laced friends and relations elsewhere.

The cemetery entrance looks like a castle, with high stone walls and arched windows. Trees rise over the crenelations as you approach the front gate. A family of three—father, mother, and son—are handing out religious pamphlets to people as they enter and exit the cemetery grounds. The little boy is dressed in his Sunday suit and plays a guitar that is almost too big for him to hold.

You decline a pamphlet, but Beatrice takes one. She reads it and frowns, then shows it to Alice before crushing it in her fist. Alice grabs the little boy's guitar from his hands. You watch her smash it on the ground.

The boy starts crying and his parents threaten to call the police. You look around and see a short line of people buying tomatoes from an old woman selling them from a basket around her neck. They are watching this scene unfold with interest.

You stare dumbly at the brides' continued antagonism of this family. When the father points to you and swears that he'll call the police and have them chop off your other arm, you box his ear so hard that he falls to the ground. His wife joins their son in tears.

You run from this family—whose day you have officially ruined—and from the brides, into the cemetery proper. You run uphill until you are out of breath, then slow down, walking through a patch of taller gravestones. You rest against one of them and turn your pockets inside out. Your mother used to make your father do that so he wouldn't bring home any ghosts. Now it's a habit.

The cemetery's narrow, paved footpaths wind through hundreds of graves and follow the rolling, uneven hills. The grass is green and lush. You curl your toes in it. Even when you forget your place and wander aimlessly, it is refreshing to see more than stones and brickwork.

Despite beginning your day with drink, you don't feel drunk. Rather, you feel neutral. Does this worry you? Are you going to look for something to push that feeling toward one extreme or the other? Of course you are. You can't let yourself exist. Or perhaps you won't.

You look down from one hill onto a clear area where families eat together on blankets. Old men walk their dogs along a stone-laden path. They are poor, but well-kempt, not homeless. A lock within you unbolts and you take a deep, unlabored breath through your nose. No one looks twice at you up there, lonely, disheveled, numb. Why would they? Treating a cemetery as a public park is already so transgressive that it doesn't allow much room for further offense.

You find the brides further along, kicking a knitted footbag between them and trying to keep it from touching the ground. You try to walk past them, but Beatrice kicks the bag to you. You feel compelled to return it, which is all they need.

You try to keep up with them, but your contributions to the game are limited to kicking the bag too hard, thus obligating you to retrieve it. Other than picking up the footbag should you kick it away, the only other rules you can discern are not serving the footbag to oneself and not jestering; the game is a cooperative one, so each player is charged with keeping the bag moving. The brides pass it between themselves, as nimble as faeries, illustrating how the game was supposed to be played, only for you to damn near kick the sand out of it when it comes to you.

One such kick sends the bag tumbling down a set of terraced marble steps and into the small archway of a mausoleum, bent with age. You run down to retrieve it and the brides follow you as far as the lowest step. You pick up the bag and toss it up and down. One of the seams is loose, and trace amounts of sand fill the lines in your palm. You wipe your hand on your trousers and turn to the brides.

"Come on, give us the bag and let's get back to the game," Beatrice says. Her face and voice are solemn, with none of her usual scofflaw's confidence. Alice's breaths are loud, and shallow. Clara isn't with them; she has crept up behind you and flicks one of the bars on the mausoleum's wrought-iron storm door. Both you and Alice jump.

"Don't touch the fucking bars," Alice says, her voice elevated. You can't tell if she's angry or scared. You pull Clara away from the mausoleum and the four of you return to the grassy patch, and the game.

"What was that about back there?" you ask. "You can't tell me you're afraid of mausoleums."

"Bars are for cages," Alice says, keeping her head down as she passes the bag from foot to foot. "Not for people. You don't put people in cages." She kicks the ball directly at Clara, who blocks it with her hands out of instinct.

"Can't use your hands," Alice says, "that's a penalty."

"You kicked it right at my face!" Clara says, almost pouting.

"Rules are rules," Alice says. "Beatrice? Do you agree?"

Beatrice nods. "Can't use your hands," she says. She smirks, but is still a little shaken.

For whatever reason, you decide to take up for Clara. "Now then, she's right. You did kick it at her face, that should be a penalty."

Alice's nose flares and she shoves you backwards. You stumble as the ground slopes down behind you and fall, rolling into a nearby bush. You use that as a chance to slip away again.

You leave the cemetery through the groundskeeper's entrance and jump on a horse-cart as it lurches away from the stop. It bends through the south end of the city, past lamp-lit taverns and pubs. Light spills over from the theatre district and washes over the cobblestones. Laughter peaks through the urban scuffle of steam-carriages, voices muffled by walls and doors and closed windows, the hidden electricity that is the natural consequence of people and their needs pressed into such close quarters.

That last item is the key to cities. Even when you cannot hear it, it's there in every anxious moment, every shortness of breath.

You disembark and walk in the direction of a dimly-lit street. A crew of workmen dig a pit that slopes down to your right. Their shovels rise and fall with operatic grace, and they only pause to wipe sweat from their sun-beaten faces and spit over their shoulders. A skinnier man than the rest sits on an upturned barrel and strums a guitar. You count *one two three four five six seven eight* before the melody repeats itself. The man's foot taps against the barrel on the even numbers, and you see the shovels' movement align with the pace of the guitar.

A rock flies down into the pit, then another, and you turn to see Alice with a handful of them. She throws two more before the diggers tell you to go away. Alice sticks her chin out and one of the diggers spits in her direction. Beatrice and Clara appear from dark patches between the gaslights, and you run again as they descend into the pit.

The old woman praises her bicycle for being low and simple. The ungainly penny-farthing bicycles she could have chosen for a mount are built that way for a purpose; they are vehicles that keep ladies in their place. The old woman likes the speed of her bicycle and the sound of her clothes billowing out around her.

She pedals through narrow alleys that crack and roll under her tyres and open into wider streets where dogs run and fight and scratch at their patchy fur. She rides too quickly to see the faces staring out from porches and greasy windows, the untreated sores, the redness that is equal parts drinking and crying and coarse bedding. It's too dark out to see them anyway, and she doesn't need to look at them right now. She will see them all, one by one, when it is time.

She skids to a halt beside a construction pit and leans her bicycle against one of several tall, skeletal machines on site. Policemen are scattered around, interviewing passers-by and inspecting the area. Three of them kneel around a body in the pit, and a fourth is turning a broken guitar over, covering his hands with a napkin to prevent fingerprint contamination. The steamlights shining into the pit splash their shadows out behind them.

The old woman takes small steps down the gouged-out slope into the pit, navigating the piles of construction materials as best she can. The body has been turned over onto its back; he was clearly beaten to death. While the police write down observations in their notebooks and search his pockets for identification, the old woman plucks a coin—a Westward Journey five-cent piece, no less—from behind his ear.

"Hm," she says, holding the coin up to the light. "They'll reuse this, for sure. Whatever you did to get yourself here," she says to the body at her feet, "don't do it next time."

The faces of these policemen are young, but still corrugated by stress. There is one older officer talking to possible witnesses outside of the pit; the old woman can only just see him over the lip of it.

"I thought he was asleep down there," one witness says, trailing her left hand up and down her right arm. "I catch these workmen drinking on the job all the time. I hate the way they look at me." She clears her throat. "My husband and I called down to him and he didn't respond, and then when we figured out how to turn on the light, we saw the blood."

The old woman turns back to look at the dead man's body. How long had he lived after that encounter, whatever it was? She'd only been called to retrieve his coin now, at the cusp of darkness, but he'd clearly been down there for some time.

As she walks back to her bicycle, she hears a second witness tell another policeman about suspicious persons she'd seen through her window: three strong-built women and a man with one arm, all of them dirty and wearing rags.

"Cities are not kind," the old woman says, slipping her feet onto the pedals.

You don't return to the carriage house. Instead, you wrap yourself in an old tarpaulin and sleep in an alley. Knowing that you will wake up alone, loneliness takes hold of you before sleep does.

In the morning, you make your way downtown on stiff legs, not yet having enough coin to take a steam horse-cart. The city swells in the middle, the shabby rowhomes, low coffeehouses, and dark-fronted leaving shops give way to proper storefronts and cobbled streets filled with steamcoaches and noise. Rust and dirt flake down from the undersides of glass-walled skywalks connecting the taller buildings. People, throngs of them, gossip and chatter, their bodies pressed together on the sidewalks.

You watch young boys, no older than thirteen, running alongside the steamcoaches and turning somersaults to show off for one another. Men in daycoats hold unfolded newspapers over their heads, unprepared for the afternoon's light drizzle. You, being similarly unprepared, remain wet.

An empty plant pot filled to its brim with dirt calls out to you, and you sit down at what turns out to be the north end of a public market. Stalls for food—fruit, vegetables, oysters, meat, and eggs—line one side of it, and stalls for other goods—brushes, combs, kitchenware, stationery, toys—line the other. The space between is dense with people, and the light rain has brought up a foul, river-water smell from the sewer pipes under the street.

You cross your legs in front of you to keep your bare feet off the wet ground, and rest your cupped hand on one knee. For lack of a hat or instrument case or something to keep money in, that will have to do.

A few passers-by drop coins into your hand before someone's breath whispers at the back of your neck. You turn to find Clara perched on the rim of the plant pot, smiling at you.

"So there you are," she says. "We were wondering where you ran off to. You're difficult to contain, Mr. Carey."

"Please leave," you say, remembering the sight of them descending upon that man in the construction pit.

"I will," she says, putting her hand on yours, "but not right now." Her hand is warm and smooth. "Are you out here begging?"

You look out at the people shopping, then down at the puddle growing under the plant pot. "Yes," you say. You want to pull your hand away and leave her sitting in the rain, so do it. Get up. There are plenty of public markets in the city, plenty of crowds to become anonymous in. Stop looking at your feet and move them.

Idiot.

"We lived with a beggar, once," Clara says. "A false one. He used to affect sores on his arms by pouring soap on them, then vinegar. It looked awful." Her arm snakes around your shoulder and squeezes your stump. "You're the genuine article, though."

"Where are the other two?" you ask, wriggling until she lets you go.

"Finally burying that coachman," Clara says. "They told me where, but I can't remember."

"I'm surprised they're extending him that courtesy," you say.

"They did him a service," Clara says. "Our husband and those blue-jackets would have tortured him if they'd caught up with him. We promised him we'd keep him safe from them if he brought us here, and we did. They can't get to him now."

"That's terrible," you say. A woman in a bright cotton dress drops coins into your hand, and you quickly shove them into your pocket. "And I suppose you're going to do the same to me."

"Not at all," Clara says, sounding offended. "We just wanted to see why you left, is all."

You scoff at that, as if you have the right. "You can't be serious. You kidnapped me and the circumstances in that house, from your crazy husband on down, almost killed me. Why on Earth would I stay?"

"The same reason everyone else does," Clara says. "Food and drink are free, the frolics are constant, and there aren't really any rules."

"Yes, there were," you say. "Just because they didn't make sense didn't mean they weren't rules."

"No one else has ever left once they were brought there," Clara says, lowering her voice as a man in a striped frock coat and trousers presses coins into your hand. "Naturally,

we were curious about the life you had before, the one you were in such a hurry to get back to."

"The one you took me from," you say.

"It's not much different than the other guests," Clara says.

"Yes, it is," you say, watching a group of five older children approach a fruit-seller's stall. "It's mine." The seller is bantering with another customer and doesn't see the children until just after one of them grabs two apples from the stack on his countertop.

"Stop, thief!" he yells at them as they all run through the crowd and scatter. His till is unsupervised, and by the time he returns to business, you have stolen it and wandered away. You consider that another child in that little gang was intending to steal the till, but you were just a shade faster that him today. Still, you look over your shoulder at street corners on your way to find a steam horse-cart.

As you wait for one to come by, Clara finds you. She is damp from the rain, which has let up a little bit, and grabs you as you walk away.

"We found new lodging," she says. "An abandoned shopfront, we think. Come back with me."

You say no, both inwardly and out loud, until she brushes her hair away from her forehead and her second set of eyes stares into you, through you, past all your prepared defenses.

When the horse-cart comes, you embark together for the ride back north.

The "new lodging" Clara spoke of is indeed an abandoned storefront, with a stoop out front and a torn canvas awning over the door. The interior is dark in the corners, making its dimensions hard to estimate, and it smells like the unventilated passage of time.

You fall asleep quickly, and wake up face-down on the floor, breathing in the mold creeping up through the boards. You roll over and wipe your face, rubbing eyes that won't stop itching.

Beatrice is standing at the window, taking deep bong tokes and placing knick-knacks on the sill: a shark's tooth necklace, a crude stone carving of a black goat, a baby squid preserved in a jar of formaldehyde, an open-mouthed fish skull.

Flecks of mold catch in your throat and you cough, startling Beatrice. She whips around and you cringe, expecting violence. When none comes, your body softens.

"Don't scare me like that," she says. "Almost dropped this." A yellow soap carving of a man on a high-backed throne rests in her palm. You step forward to get a better look at it.

"What is it?" you ask.

"A souvenir," Beatrice says. "They're all souvenirs. Things we took from where we've been." The smoke curling from her mouth and nose smells almost pleasant.

Even though she didn't really answer your previous question, you try another. "Where did this one come from?"

"A curiosity shop," Beatrice says, placing the sculpture on the windowsill with the other knick-knacks. "Do you have those here?"

"No," you say.

Beatrice shrugs. "They're all over the place where we're from. Overseas, I suppose you'd call it. Anyway, I took this before we came here."

Overseas is what your parents and their farmhands and the other laboring men call the collection of cities and towns on the other side of a wide, gray ocean. You've only seen that ocean once, during a rare family vacation to a rocky piece of coastline hours east of the farm. Your father has been there once before and said the people Overseas are peculiar, that their cities are blasphemous constructions of iron and glass.

"I've never been Overseas," you say. "I've heard things, but I've never been." You pick up the sculpture yourself, surprised that Beatrice didn't stop you. "This feels like tallow soap," you say, rubbing your thumb over the details. "He looks like a king."

"In a sense," Beatrice says. "There aren't really kings anymore. Too hard to concentrate power. Too many people." She takes the sculpture from you and puts it back on the sill next to the bottled squid. "This one is from home," she says, indicating the squid. "Alice plucked it out of the water right before we left."

"What did the Count think of it?" you ask.

"We hadn't met him yet," Beatrice says. "Wouldn't meet him for a long time. We were children when we left home."

You pick up the bottle and squint, moving it around to get a closer look at the thing inside. The squid has aged into a colorless mass, tentacles drooping, eyes milky and cold.

"Children?"

"Yes," Beatrice says, lighting the bong again, not offering it to you. "Our parents were all sent to debtor's prison. No one else could raise us, so we could either starve to death in the ratty little canal town we came from, or try our luck out in the world."

"That's very brave," you say. You would have never left home as a child. You had to pry yourself away as an adult, and look where that got you.

"I don't like that word," Beatrice says. "The only people who say things like 'brave' and 'noble' and 'hero' are people who aren't willing to help."

"I would have helped," you say. You sound, and are, insincere.

Beatrice snorts. "Don't be stupid. You wouldn't have even noticed us."

"How do you know?"

"Because no one notices you." Her words sting as they land home. When you scrounge and beg for money, even the people who drop coins at your feet don't look at you. They focus straight ahead, jaws set, shoulders squared. They turn away from you on public benches and walk past in silence as you pick through gutters and trash barrels and stormwater drains. When policemen shoo you away, it's no more than they would give a stray animal.

"It was a mistake, being born a woman," Beatrice says. The smoke she exhales has soured. "I should have been a virus. I could have done some good in the world and cut down the population to something manageable."

You ignore that and pick up the black stone goat. The tail moves, and makes the familiar clicking sound of a winding key. You turn it around and around until the goat's belly slides open, revealing a glass eye. In your shock, you drop the goat. Beatrice swoops down and grabs it, inspecting it carefully before putting it back on the sill. Before you can apologize, she leaves.

The smell of meat wakes you up, and you are summoned to a hot meal of beef pie with sauce and a jug of beer, courtesy of the brides. You don't ask where they got it, nor do you eat as much as you should. The oil and muck from your dirty fingers stains the sauce. The brides pick out sections of pie with their hands, forgoing the sauce and beer altogether, leaving them to you.

"This city has so many old people in it," Alice says, alternating between a handful of beef pie and the bong's mouthpiece.

"So?" you ask.

"They're too old," Alice says. "People weren't meant to live so long." She passes the bong to Beatrice, who nods and accepts it.

"You should die when your body does," Beatrice says. "Keeping yourself alive beyond that is just vanity, and fear. It's horrid." She pauses to swallow a belch. "And selfish. Die when your time comes and make space for the young."

"That's awfully easy for you to say," you tell her, as beer loosens your tongue. "You married rich. What are the rest of us supposed to do? Once a man's done working, he's entitled to rest and enjoy himself."

"Death is rest, you idiot," Beatrice says, swatting Clara's hand out of the way and grabbing more pie. "And how much joy is there in old age, really?" She flicks grease off her fingers. "Waiting for your brain to shut down before your body rots around it. It's pathetic."

"The Count seems to be enjoying himself just fine," you say.

"Then it's not his time yet," Alice says, blowing smoke up toward the ceiling. Little bits of meat fleck out of her mouth. "I'm starting to wonder if he's even of this Earth. The man's constitution is downright alien."

"Why don't you ask Clara?" Beatrice asks with a cruel smile after a deep toke. "She's the one who sleeps with him."

Clara snatches the bong from Beatrice's hand and scowls at her as Alice laughs. "You're both mean," she says, her face blurry in the smoke. "I shouldn't have to do that." She pulls from the bong again, and starts coughing. The three of you wait for her to stop, but she doesn't. She drops the bong and bends over as it rolls away from her. Her eyes bulge, her face fills with blue, the saucepot gets kicked over.

Alice grabs the bong and quickly tokes before Beatrice can get to it. She blows smoke through a grin that fades with impatience.

"Well don't just sit there," she says to you. "Help her. She's choking." Her voice lacks urgency.

"What if it's her time?" you can't help asking.

"You're the one saying people should live longer," Alice says.

Beatrice pulls Clara up to her feet and guides you behind her. "Wrap your arm around her," she says. You do. "Make a fist under her ribs." You do.

"Now push the—oh. You don't have a second arm for that. How tragic." Beatrice laughs and passes the bong back to Alice as they watch you pump Clara's chest with your lone fist. She sputters, drools, her arms going slack. You and your impotent little arm are failing.

You pull her close to you and run into the wall, hoping the resistance will push your fist up and dislodge whatever is stuck in her throat. It does. She half-vomits a clump of beef pie against the wall and pulls away from you, retching and spitting. You don't realize how hard you're breathing until she calms down and all you can hear is yourself.

Clara kneels down and Beatrice stands behind her, brushing her hair. Alice stares at you, blowing smoke in your face through that grin of hers.

"Do you know what old men do?" she asks. "They build prisons to keep younger men like cattle, and factories to work them like slaves." She looks over at the other two and rolls her eyes. "There's no wisdom in it, just greed and fear." She looks down at the mostly-eaten pie. "The rest is yours," she says as she walks outside and slams the door behind her.

You finish the jug of beer later that night. The pie grows moldy over the next few days.

The old woman's first appointment today is in a well-appointed home on the eastern end of the city; a wealthy patriarch's coin has come up for collection. The old woman creeps into his bedroom, as invisible to his weeping family as their servants.

The sheets of this patriarch's canopy bed are pulled up to his chin; only his shriveled, discolored head is visible. Light floods the room through three large windows, their curtains thin and black. His desk is cluttered, and likely hasn't been touched since he last used it.

A small orange cat wanders into the room, rubbing against the feet of the bed before jumping into one of the room's brittle-looking chairs. The old woman snorts and looks away.

"See, you have a cat," she says to the patriarch. "I bet it knocked things off your desk and sharpened its claws on your furniture." She folded her arms. "And jumped in your lap just to look up at your face."

As she takes the dead man's coin, she wonders if anyone in his family saw her. It's not something she's used to worrying about. She isn't sure how to process it, and the cat curling itself into a tight little ball is only complicating her feelings at the moment.

That one-armed man was the second to have seen her without occult help. The first was a fat gondolier who saw her as his boat drifted by the house of a woman who'd died of cholera. She can't remember what he said to her, or vice versa, but they had shared words. Hers were most likely impolite.

What she does remember is collecting his coin from a pauper's hospital. He'd been shrunk down to nothing by poor health, his bones visible through loose flaps of skin. She regrets never talking to him, never getting his story and divining how he'd gained the eyes to see her.

She will not let that chance slip away twice, she decides. One way or another, she will have an audience with this one-armed man.

In the chair, the cat stretches a hind leg and purrs.

"Stop that," she tells it. "It's not making this any easier." The cat ignores her, as cats do.

Alice finds a fat little raccoon digging through the trash piled up in what had been the shop's storage closet, and swings it against the wall by its tail. Beatrice howls with laughter. Clara allows herself a smile as she smashes out the shop's few unbroken windows. Beatrice tells you that she wants to see what a raccoon's heart looks like. She's never seen one before. Alice has, and won't tell her anything.

The object you pull from the raccoon's chest is warm and slick with blood, and the size of a chestnut. You stare at it in your hand until Beatrice snatches it away from you. Alice grabs your hand and wipes the raccoon's blood on her face as Beatrice runs off with the heart. You lift the raccoon by its tail and toss it into the street.

"Why did you do that?" you ask Alice, exasperated.

Alice shrugs. "If you want to get through this life, you're going to have to hurt people. And if you're going to have to hurt people, you might as well enjoy it."

"That was a raccoon," you say, pointing at its body in the street.

"Call it practice," Alice says. "Besides, you pulled its heart out."

She's right. You did.

The old woman rides through a puddle and feels the spray against her calf, wonders if it will leave a stain.

She'd been to that abandoned storefront again. The three women and the one-armed man were playing cards on the floor, and the old woman had studied him through the window. He spoke little, and when he did speak it brought sharp rebukes or physical violence upon him from his companions.

The women, meanwhile, had observed the amount of abandoned buildings in the city, and compared it to other cities they'd lived in where wealthy men bought up the land under such buildings and subtracted its value from whatever amount they were required to pay back into their communities. Blight made these men wealthier, they said without a trace of outrage.

The man asked if their shared husband, Drogado, had made such arrangements, and was bullied into silence. He could have left at any point, the old woman thinks. He could have stood up and walked out. And yet, he stayed. One of the women made a show of brushing her arm against his and touching his hand, and flashing coquettish smiles at him, but they did little to alleviate his obvious pain.

The old woman's mind snaps back to the present as the street bends around a boxy church whose garden creeps under the fence surrounding it, onto the sidewalk. She imagines the sweating preacher inside, the congregation of paddle fans and squirming children in mended rags, their inaccurate perception of her. Her skirts jingle as her legs move.

If only they knew that they do not have souls. They have bodies. They share souls.

Alice follows you down a narrow alley, stepping over the bits of trash you kick to the side without stopping. The two of you walk under rusted metal fire escapes that could collapse at any moment, and past the rotted shell of a steamcoach. The engine, tyres, and anything of practical value were stripped from it long ago. The rear window is cracked, but not broken until Alice finds a chunk of concrete and smashes it.

The alley ends in a forbidding courtyard penned in by abandoned buildings, their entrances bricked up. Rude words and symbols have been chalked onto every flat surface, and a thick mat of weeds has grown up through the pavement. You watch Alice cover her nose. When you first arrived in the city, the odor of dead things mingling with the city's temperamental sewer system brought tears to your eyes at least once a day. You've come so far since then.

Turning left, you squeeze through a crack between two buildings, ending up on a wider street where a few other people sit in groups, passing cigarettes and bottles among themselves under a pale sky that washes everything out.

The liquor store is on your immediate right. Neglect has tinted its once-clear windows a strange amber color.

"We walked all this way for liquor?" Alice asks as she follows you inside.

"This place will sell to me," you say, referencing your shabby appearance, made shabbier by the black dust on the floor. You leave tracks behind you as you peruse the low shelves, spinning unlabeled glass bottles to observe their contents.

"Any place will sell to me, you idiot," Alice says. "You could have just sent me into a proper shop and waited outside." She snorts. "Not only are you a terrible drunk, you're terrible at *being* a drunk."

You don't respond. She's right, anyway. This shop is on the lowest of the low end, and no larger than a corner. From the tiny counter, the clerk—wearing a tinted goggle over his right eye—frowns at you both. You select a bottle that doesn't have too much sediment floating in it and pay him in coins without a word exchanged between the two of you. You prefer it that way. The idea of a "proper shop," with lights and enthusiastic clerks and friendly chatter, fills you with dread.

Back on the street, you take a long dram from the bottle. Alice fidgets, waiting for you. Her sisters have the bong, and its absence makes her uncomfortable.

"There's no water here," she says, as you wipe your lips. You offer the bottle to her and she refuses.

"Not to drink. Look." She gestures around as you start walking again. "It's all bricks and stones here. No water."

"So?"

"I grew up on the water," Alice says. "A river, anyway. It's a much better way to live." A haggard fellow in a brown coat asks the two of you for cigarettes and Alice punches him in the face. The blow knocks him into the street, and Alice drags you away when you offer him the bottle.

"Don't bother," she says. Her voice is scratchier than it was a moment ago. "What was I saying?"

"The water."

"Yes." She nods, wiping her hand on her dress. "It's a better way to live than this. Even for someone like you."

"If the water is so great, why did you leave it?" you ask, the liquor glowing hot in your belly. "And why did you settle in the country? There's no water around Drogado's house for miles."

"We're not settled," Alice says, and you tense in anticipation of a punch or slap from her. She doesn't even look your way. You're almost insulted by that. Her fists are clenched, though, and she's tensing as much as you are. Broken-down houses with barred windows loom over the sidewalk to your left, with more of the same across the street. The yellowing front yards have grown together between some of these houses.

"Why'd you leave, then?" you ask, taking another drink. Your gums and throat ache.

"We had to," Alice says, "but we stuck close to the ocean. It's calming. We used to run around on beaches as children, even in the winter, and pop jellyfish that washed up in the high tide."

"Pop them?"

"With rocks." Alice smiles. "Sometimes I would stare out at it, watching the pelicans dive for fish as the waves broke, and think about the water coming in more and more and raising higher and higher, until that's all there was." She clears her throat, suddenly aware of how hoarse she's gotten. "That, and the sound the water makes. It's like breathing."

"Are you less violent near the water?" you ask, the bottle swinging from between your pointer and middle fingers. "Minus the jellyfish, I mean."

"Am I too violent now?" Alice asks.

"You punched someone who just wanted a cigarette," you say. You don't bring up anything she's done to you, even though it scrolls through your mind until you take a long swig from the bottle. The effects of that liquor hit you all at once, and you stop and lean against the chain fence surrounding what remains of a small, one-story house.

Alice stops and takes the bottle from you. She holds it up against the sky, swirling the contents around and watching them settle before smashing the bottle on the ground. You hate her for it, but can't stop her. Your stomach burns.

"No one ever just wants a cigarette," she says, picking up the broken neck end of the bottle. "Once you give them something, they'll take until you make them stop." She carves a rut into the fence with the jagged end of the bottle. "Knowing that I can make them stop is relaxing, too."

You don't believe that. Or rather, you know that she hurts people on a whim. You've seen it, and felt it. Your mind swirls with those thoughts, and your stomach tightens. By the time you open your mouth to rebut her, all you can do is dry heave.

What does she think you want? What *do* you want?

You watch from the window as a man strolls past the brides, who are passing their bong between themselves on the stoop. The trousers of the man's one-piece boilersuit are tucked into rubberized boots, and his mustache and beard are untrimmed. His face is creased with worry.

"Sir?" Clara asks, in the precise tone of voice that obligates a response. "You look troubled. Is everything all right?"

"Nothing to trouble you with, ma'am," the man says. "Just having a bit of a walk."

"Have a bit of a smoke, too," Clara says. She holds the bong in her lap and breathes freely in the gloom hanging over their heads. "Maybe it will clear your head." She shares glances with Beatrice and Alice.

The man has no response, says nothing. His face tenses in that silence. "I shouldn't, ma'am. You have a good evening, then."

"Oh, come now," Clara says, sweeping the hair back from her forehead, exposing her third and fourth eyes. "Just one." The man is transfixed, the same way you were, and are. Your face erupts in phantom tics as you watch his fall into that stupid, willing expression. After some hesitance, he accepts the bong from Clara. His eyes roll back in his head as he takes a deep toke.

Alice and Beatrice lean forward, watching him. Clara looks back at the window and you duck down. She may have seen you there. Your body floods with nervous warmth.

"My wife," the man says, "is ill, off and on. Our first child weakened her, though he is tall and strong. She wants another child, but I'm unsure." His breathing labors. His fists tighten. "I'm afraid another child would kill her."

Beatrice takes the bong from him and makes a suggestive display of putting her mouth to it.

"Don't you have a priest to guide you through these decisions?" she asks.

"He would tell me to have another child, of course," the man says. "Children are a blessing on the household, and all that."

"Are you guessing what he would say, or do you know?"

"I haven't asked him," the man admitted. "He has no wife or children. He speaks from the Scriptures, not his own heart."

Smoke spills out of Beatrice's mouth. A young boy zips by on a bicycle.

"What is the point of having children," Beatrice says, "without the privilege of raising them?" She smirks. "And why raise them at all? At best, they will be scavengers, picking meat from the bones of a dying planet."

The man sputters a little. "Excuse me?"

"Look around you," she says, with a sweep of her arm. "Do you think any of this is going to stop?"

An omnibus trumpets past. Its windows catch and bend light from the gaslamps. Above them, the terraced roofline of old, dirty buildings makes a horizon, and the square hulks of factories and mills loom over it. Brick chimneys rise up into the sky, blackening it with soot and creosote.

"I think I'd best be going," the man says, but Alice wraps her arm around his throat and holds him still.

"Every day, the sun gets colder," Beatrice says. "The moon pulls the oceans further away from us. The ground hollows out under our feet. And yet we expect to conquer the wilderness. We're stupid. People are so stupid."

The man struggles in Alice's grip, his face turning red; she claps a hand over his mouth. Again, Clara looks to the window. Again, you shrink away. Excitement and dread course through you, tingling your fingers and toes.

"Do you really want to make another piece of meat for a world that will just crush it?" Beatrice asks. The man kicks at her, yelling incoherently behind Alice's hand. She lets him go and he springs away, stumbling on the sidewalk. Alice is right on top of him, and punches him dead in the face before he can react. He drops to his side and covers up as best as he can.

"Go home and eliminate it," Beatrice says. Alice kicks him again before he scrambles away. Through all this, Clara sits as still and silent as a pond, her head tilted at the same angle as her smile.

The last time you saw your mother smile, you were eight years old. You'd made up a dance and performed it for her in the kitchen, your feet attempting rhythm in your rigid church shoes. Your mother clapped along, her airy laughter wrapping around you like a blanket.

This moment was interrupted by your father, who came in from the fields and watched you for a moment before telling you to "stop clattering around like a scared horse." If you had energy to spend, he told you, then you should put your boots on and get to work.

After she stopped smiling, your mother grew distant from other pleasures. Her knitting needles and yarn gathered dust on the shelf. The pages in her books withered away. Her appetite became a routine. Sitting between their wintry faces at the breakfast table, you learned that work and prayer are the only two stones in the path between the crib and the grave.

The brides insist that you play a game called "No One Is Dressed Without a Smile." Clara explains the rules, which are simple. One member of the group is allowed to smile, and can do whatever they like to get another player to smile; should they succeed, that other player is "it." The player who resists smiling for the duration of the game is the winner.

The game spills out of the abandoned storefront and into the street, where Alice grins as she pulls a bird from its nest and snaps it neck. Beatrice smiles and runs barefoot along the cobblestones, tickling her sisters as it pleases her and screaming vulgarities at full voice into the empty sky. "Cunt!" you remember her yelling. "Fucking dirty cunt!"

Her language forces a smile from Clara, who turns her attention to you. She asks her sisters how they should make you smile, and Beatrice tells Alice to beat it out of you. Alice pulls stones up from the street and throws them at you. You run, of course. The rows of buildings on either side of you flatten out into empty lots. You run toward the city's skyline as stones, bottles, and other debris land at your heels, imagining the shape of those distant buildings as massive teeth rooted into a monstrous jaw that would open and swallow you and everything you'd ever seen.

Your limbs loosen and you spread the fingers on your remaining hand. You can almost feel the freefall as you disappear into the endless gullet of something beyond all reckoning. At last, the conceits of this world would be broken.

A half-brick tags the back of your head and you stumble onto the ground, as real as it was before you wished it weren't.

Moments later, Alice and Beatrice kick you with the blades of their feet, grinding into your bones with their heels. Clara lowers herself to your ear, whispering pleas to smile and end this game.

"Winning is impossible, and thus unimportant," she says. "Besides, you owe us a smile." As new gardens of pain bloom within your body, she begs you to surrender.

"Please," she says, stroking your cheek. "For me. For yourself."

You roll over onto your back and endure kicks to your sides, sternum, and testicles. Overhead, the sky is a gray

mirror of clouds. Your face is blank. Your nose and eyes and mouth recede.

Alice and Beatrice slow their abuse, then stop altogether. "It's no use," Alice says, disappointed. "He's too good at this." Clara helps you to your feet, also disappointed. She supports you as the four of you retrace your steps back to the storefront.

Along the way, Beatrice stuffs a dirty rag into an unmarked brown bottle and lights it on fire. She hands it to Alice. "Throw it through that window," she says, pointing to an unremarkable brick building that could have been a house, or a tenement, or a hundred other inconsequential things. Her third eye is open, and she brushes her hair away from it with her hand.

Alice throws it, and after a few moments you see flames and smoke licking up past the windowsill.

If someone asked you what made your father laugh, you wouldn't know what to tell them. The closest he came to expressing joy was when he stuffed explosives under stumps on the family property and blew them up. He would always let the remnants smolder for a few moments before stomping them out. His eyes allowed a light that was much different than the one reflected by the fire.

Whenever it was necessary to burn brush or leaves, he never allowed you or your mother to participate. You two would wait inside and watch his formless silhouette through the kitchen window as he watched the flames reach higher and higher. In good weather, he would feed that fire for hours, not letting it die until well after you and your mother had fallen asleep.

The inside of the building glows orange as the four of you stand there, Clara bending under your weight. The air thickens with smoke. You hear voices and muffled cries from the upper levels of the building, which cues the brides to turn and continue walking back to the storefront.

You feel one side of your mouth curl up, and surrender to it.

A sharp pain awakens you. Alice laughs.

"I told you to kick him," Beatrice says.

"I improvised," is Alice's reply.

The old woman follows this one-armed man as he walks through the city on bare feet. She is careful not to get too close, a concession she's never had to make before, and one which causes her some discomfort.

The man pays a penny to ride a clockwork horse cart downtown, and she watches him rummage through trash barrels and bins, pulling coins and scraps of food from them with keen nimbleness. Had circumstances been different, the old woman thinks, he would have done well at her job.

He walks with his shoulders slumped and his back curved, his head tilted down, and a gas-motored shopcart almost collides with him as he crosses a busy street. The old woman has to skid to an undignified halt behind a fallen awning to avoid being seen. The awning belongs to a shop whose owner has repaired it before, and he comes out swearing and cursing at it for falling down again. As he leans a wooden ladder against the wall and walks back inside to gather tools, she resumes following the one-armed man.

The man picks coins from a small wishing well in a patch of grass between two drab, brownstone buildings and gets chased off by a policeman. He continues on, walking down a hill without sufficient cover to hide the old woman, who halts at the top of the hill for a moment. He turns back and she runs off, deciding to take a parallel street and hoping it meets up with the man at the bottom of the hill. She splays her legs out as she coasts down, her pedals spinning, her tyres bouncing against the cobblestones.

Her official duties nag at her as she rides further down the street, looking for a way to cross back and find that one-armed-man again. There are still coins to be collected. Even one such as she, who understands the true cubic nature of time and the malleability thereof, can still waste it.

She turns to bike through a coach gate that becomes a covered alley, and rides up the solid concrete steps. Before her front tyre touches the steps, she sees a beggar woman sitting with her back against the wall. She is pulled into herself. Her head is bowed and she is whispering. The old woman can't tell if she is praying or crying, if her hands are gnarled around rosary beads, if the tears salting her palms and nailbeds are born of worship.

When she emerges back onto the proper street, the one-armed-man is gone. The old woman curses and spits, then rides back up the hill towards the first of today's coins to be collected.

The ground puckers its lips and blows you into the air. The tops of the mill chimneys disappear and blue drains from the sky as you soar higher and higher, eventually losing contact with the windspout and drifting up. The sun's belly passes over you and begins its descent at the exact moment your ascent peaks.

Your body is an autumn leaf rocked in the cradle of the wind. Below you are thousands of terraced cityscapes, awake with light. The sun burns the sky a brilliant orange as it sets, and the cities grow taller and wider. Roads unspool and overlap, fire escapes climb the sides of steel towers that light from within. Skybridges arc above the clouds and connect these towers.

Tiny specks converge upon these cities as the sun's blush consumes the sky. The clouds dissolve as foul smoke spreads under your feet. It slows your fall, leaving ash and creosote behind as you pass through it. The sky is red now. You hear coughing and screaming down below, then wailing laments as the cities rise to meet you. They absorb the light, and you cannot look at them for long. Laments become gunshots, then explosions, then noises you cannot name.

The sun rolls behind the horizon, leaving a burgundy sky behind, and the smoke you fell through turns to rain. The heat against your skin comes from fire down below, the kind that can't be put out. Smoke rises and hardens into coral that shines like glass. Amid the sounds of human violence, rain beats the cities down into sloping dunes, and by the time you're halfway to the ground again, dirty water has worn them down and made lace of them.

You land on a blanket of bones that spreads out as far as you can see in every direction. As soon as you gather your footing, the bones pull you in. As you sink, roots stretch and swell and the bodies of trees rise past you. When they break through into the open air, there will be no sun to greet them. You know this, though you aren't sure how.

Are you calm, or just numb? You have not struggled to fight or understand anything you've seen. Your body is limp as gravity pulls it deeper into this ocean of bones. You are aware of your breath expanding your stomach, but what good is that now? Why breathe and do nothing with it? Kick your legs. Swing your arm. Resist. Fight, damn you. Show your father's bones, wherever they are, that he raised a man after all.

You smell algae and salt, and are submerged in water. You flail in the water, desperate to break the surface, but that only makes you sink faster. The bones thin out until there are none left, and you are floating in water the color of a dead and broken sun. You bash yourself against rocks and undersea cliffs and when you reach the sea floor, you burst through it.

At last you land, and you recognize your surroundings immediately; you are in Count Drogado's mansion, on the floor of the room you first met him in. Water drips down from a hole in the ceiling above you.

A tree has grown through the center of the house. Its branches have shattered the windows and walls. Flowers pop open along the tree's bark and new plants sprout up through the floor. You hear insects buzzing and see pollen drifting in the air, made visible by dim, cold light. Vines curl through the open spaces of a skeleton lying near what you can see of the tree; as you watch, they pull the bones tight against the bark.

You wake up with a start, just as Clara pulls away from your ear. You can still hear her voice ringing in your head. A dream is all that was.

Your breath expands your stomach, filling it with the storefront's stale air. The brides have gathered next to you, and you drowsily accept the communal bong when it is offered. You toke deeply from your knees before rising to your feet, letting the rush of blood to your head tumble against the smoke filling it with gloom.

"Sit back down," Alice says. "We're going to play Forfeit." Clara claps her hands and smiles.
You ask how to play, and they explain, as the bong passes between the three of them, that one person leaves the room while the others select something of value to

them and place it in the center of the room. When the person who left the room reenters, he or she becomes the "auctioneer" of these items. The brides' enthusiasm for this part of the game is obvious, even to you. You shield your eyes from the meager sunlight. Your face throbs whenever light touches it.

Alice slaps your hand away as Beatrice explains that in order to keep from "forfeiting" your item, you must do something embarrassing to win it back. All three of them smile at this, and their eyes glaze black, even Beatrice's third eye.

"Like what?" you ask, curling away from the light.

"Like sing a song, or dance, or tell us a story," Clara says, looking at your stump. She announces that she will be the first auctioneer and skips out into the street.

Alice and Beatrice cast a necklace and a pair of white lace gloves into the center of the room. When they turn to you, you compress until your knees touch your chest.

"I don't have anything," you say. Alice pulls you up to your feet by your ear, and they examine you. Shame flushes through you.

"You must have something," Beatrice says, as she plunges her hands in and out of your pockets. Alice grabs handfuls of loose skin and pulls, forces your mouth open with dirty fingers to look inside, picks through your unwashed hair. Beatrice's fingers brush against your thighs as Clara knocks on the door, wondering if she can

be let in yet. Alice shouts at her to hold her horses, then pushes you into the center of the circle.

She produces a knife from her skirts and invites Clara back into the room, whereupon she stabs you in the stomach. Pain, then a calm and soothing emptiness, expands within you.

"What we have here," Alice says, as you adjust to what is happening to you, "is the life of one Thomas Carey, who refuses the hospitality of our husband, despite our attempts to renew his invitation." She pushes the knife in a little deeper. "A man who courts oblivion until it appears on his doorstep." She sneers at you; all you can muster in response is disbelief.

"What are my bids for this item?" Clara is beaming, her posture thrust up to the ceiling.

As Beatrice and Alice squabble over what they would bid for your life, you watch them as though from a distance. You can see every particle of smoke in the air. Specks of dust gleam in the sunlight. The brides' voices degrade into pure sound, with no articulation. The emptiness you felt before has spread through your limbs and up into your chest. Your heart slows to a stop.

Clara grabs your shoulder and shakes it from a hundred miles away. Your bones shake as the blade pulls out of your belly. You feel blood running down under your trousers as the brides and the room and the world outside of it return to you.

"He's supposed to tell a story first!" Clara says. A clump of Alice's hair dangles from her hand. "You saw him! One moment longer and he'd have been dead." Clara is angrier than you've ever seen her. Alice has a swollen lip. Beatrice wedges herself between them.

"He owes us a story, then," she says, "and then Alice gets to beat him for almost dying on us." They speak of you as they would an object.

Clara kneels down in front of you, her hands resting on her legs. Blood oozes through your shirt and trousers, humid against your skin. She takes your hand in hers. "What was the last thing you did before you lost your arm?" All four of her eyes meet yours.

At first, you refuse the question rather inelegantly, but Alice reminds you of the penalty for not playing along. Your mind refuses to focus, and you shut your eyes to aid concentration. In fits and starts, you tell the brides the last thing you did with two arms.

Some of the men in the workhouse decided to unionize and strike for better pay and food, and management offered the rest of you extra money to break their strike. You were one of those who took them up on it.

You didn't recognize any of the other men who gathered in that windowless shed on the workhouse's property. They were a rough lot, what the press would later call a goon squad, but truthfully they were no different than the men they were being paid to beat. Even the alcoholics, criminals, and hard-bitten losers who would do nearly anything for cash on the hogshead were still working men. So were you, once upon a time. Unfortunately, at that moment the only unifying element among you was failure, and what better career for failed men than to inhibit those who dare to succeed?

The actual violence was swift, and the strike only lasted two days. Your arms kept an axe-handle busy for less than an hour that afternoon, and then three weeks later one of them was ripped away by circumstance. Good riddance, really.

You have since learned that strikes are social, that they reinforce identity. Now divorced from any direct engagement with strikers, you see them as an observer, hear their voices in the street, watch them picket and march before imposing brick mill buildings and crumbling tenements. They are dirty, down at the heel, and yet they shine.

It is hard to watch strikers and not wonder if any of them recognize you.

Picture your parents' faces when you told them you'd taken a strikebreaking job. They would ask why, of course. Would you have answered? Can you answer now? They can't hear you or cast doubt on your reasoning. They're gone. Whatever you thought you were protecting them from, it wasn't death. If you wanted to prove something to them, you never let them see what it was.

That is what you tell the brides. Tears roll down your face as you finish.

The brides let you fall asleep where you sit. Alice kindly welshes on her promise to beat you. You nod off to the sound of the brides squealing with delight outside, crushing rats under their bare heels.

When you wake up, they are gone.

The brides are missing.

You sleep through that first day, grateful for the silence. Beyond one tense moment when you think someone, a stranger, was staring in through one of the windows, it is the most peaceful day you've had in ages.

You wake late in the night, unable to return to sleep, and that's when the idleness creeps into your stupid

weak heart, and you pine for them. For all they
bring out in you, for all their violence and gleeful
maliciousness, you cannot deny the shadow they've cast
over you. Clearly you haven't made peace with the idea
of being lonely and empty.

You stare across that dirty room, adjusting to a darkness
that had been freeing, and is now crushing. You drag your
heel back and forth on the floor, worrying a trench into
the grime. Such energy, wasted. It is the folly of men to
spend themselves so fully on trivial things. By the time
you're old enough to understand what really matters,
you're too tired to pursue it.

On the second day, you leave your illegal lodging and
find yourself near the university. A priest has organized
twelve of his flock into a line that extends from one
side of its imposing stone entrance to the other. Two
of them bear lanterns, despite the daylight and heat.
They have picked an especially humid day to make
a spectacle, so they all shine with sweat. The priest's
black sleeves are rolled up to his elbows, and the hair
on his thick forearms is matted down.

They all hold hands and sing hymns; the priest's voice is
strong, but not tuneful, and he rears his head back to belt out
Here I Am, Lord and *Bring Flowers of the Rarest* and *At the Lamb's
High Feast We Sing.* The others sing along as best they can,
even though a couple of them have trouble remembering
the words without a hymnal. Their 'voices shrink with
hesitance in those moments, and their eyes lower out of
habit, squinting to read words that aren't there.

You feel bad for them in that moment, you really do. You know how that feels.

When the priest stops to speak about faith and forbearance and the moral duty of citizens to love their neighbors, he either stares up at the high stone archway that is the university's entrance, or down toward the unevenly cobbled road, squeezed narrow by old buildings now reserved for the students and professors and their needs.

Two pretty girls are passing out religious tracts, showing their teeth when they smile. You take a pamphlet from them, but lose it on the way back home. Your mother would say that it turned into a bird in your pocket and flew away. That's what she said whenever anyone lost anything. Thinking of her compels you to beat your head against the wall until your forehead splits open. You fold back down onto your side as blood masks your face.

You wake up on the third day with searing pain in your ribs, and swelling on your forehead. You bear it as long as you can, then embrace your weakness and make your way to the city hospital. The clockwork horse carts are all crowded, and you should have taken more precautions to protect other passengers from your disgusting, broken body. You don't, though. Of course.

One would think that the neighborhoods around the hospital, a scrubbed-white pillar of modern medicine, would be upscale, but thereupon lies one of the city's great practical jokes: the hospital is surrounded by squalor. The roads are cracked and pitted, with dirt floor alleys serving as cross streets, and many of the buildings are boarded up. What strikes you hardest about the area is how empty it is. Apart from the whistles and bells of passing ambulances, the only signs of life are small, unfriendly corner shops and the occasional drunk passed out on the front steps of a shuttered rowhouse.

The hospital itself is an imposing archipelago of white buildings and close-cropped lawns with stone pathways indicating where to walk. When you disembark, your first step onto the pavement whips pain up into your ribs, and you drop to a knee. Your mouth fills with spit, and you at least have the courtesy to empty it into the grass instead of the sidewalk.

A hand brushes against yours and helps you to your feet. Your eyes meet two of Clara's, which are shiny and bright. "We're going to play hide-and-seek," she tells you. "I can't," you say. "I need to see a doctor."

"No you don't," she says.

"My ribs," you say as they throb, "they're broken. And the cut on my forehead. I don't have time for a game right now." A vacuum has formed between your brain, which knows this to be true, and your heart, which is swelling at the sight of Clara. It stirs your words into mud. They lack conviction.

"We're the only reason you're even alive," Beatrice says, startling you. "You fell to pieces without us. We should have left you for dead." She snarls at you, her third eye invisible. Clara's hair is drawn in front of her third and fourth eyes.

"Besides," Alice says, appearing suddenly to your left, "you found us. It's your turn to hide now." Blood rims her fingernails.

"He doesn't want to play," Beatrice says.

"I can't play," you say, raising your voice. "I'm dying."

"Of course you are," Clara says. "A little more every day." Her arm slithers around your shoulder and turns you away from the hospital.

Beatrice flanks you on the right. "I should find a big rock so Alice can bash his head in," she says.

"Not before we play hide-and-seek," Alice says, walking in front as they lead you down the street to wait for a clockwork horse cart. Whenever you resist or struggle, she steps on your heels, herding you the way dogs guide sheep into pens. Fitting, really.

You and the brides disembark from the horse cart into a different neighborhood, showing more vital signs than where you'd been squatting before. Sun-bleached, narrow

row homes with plain brick facades fence in the street. Weeds sprawl out from the edges of the sidewalks. You can hear city traffic in the distance.

The brides sit down on the wooden bench of an omnibus stop. They tell you that you have until the count of one hundred to hide. They shut their eyes and begin counting in sing-song unison.

You run. You run as fast as you can down the street, swatting flies from your face with your free hand. An empty trash barrel on the sidewalk looks like it could accommodate you, and you move it behind a nearby bush to make it less conspicuous. As soon as you've nudged it into place, you step inside, only to find that you can still hear them counting. Can you really? Or is this an aberration of the mind? Either way, you step out of the barrel and keep running.

You dash past a neighborhood laundry where a group of old women in green dresses scrub clothes in washtubs that overflow with suds. They flap the clothes out in the sludgy afternoon air: a white shirt with pale buttons, slim black trousers with tapered legs. Your exact costume, down to the smallest detail, even the ragged trouser hems.

You grab their washtub and pour the soapy water into the street, intending to hide under it, but what if those old hags tell the brides where you are? One of them spits at your feet as you flee, leaving the tub overturned.

Houses fade out into an open area for merchant stalls that, unattended, looks like any other vacant lot in the city. At the sight of these unmanned stalls, you feel the count approaching one hundred in your bones.

There's a way out of this, you know. Don't act like you haven't thought about it every day. That's the one place they can't find you. The oblivion you seek is all around you, beckoning you in. Why do you resist? At least the pain you would endure has a definite end to it, unlike the stasis your life has become. Hurt, eat, hurt, drink, hurt, sleep. Hurt one final time and be done with it. Welcome the abyss like a lover, like a friend returning home.

You pound on the door of a nearby house, having seen signs of occupancy. No one answers, but the door is unlocked. You enter and slam the door behind you. The lock mechanism has been removed, and blood streaks the walls of the narrow hallway leading into the belly of the house.

Dead. They are all dead. The children, too.

You leave the same way you entered. A black steamcoach idles in the street in front of the house. The front end and side have been punched in from when it smashed into the tree during your escape from Count Drogado's house.

This time, you don't even have time to run. Clara wraps her arms around you and kisses you fully on the mouth. Her voice echoes in your head. Found you.

Here comes a candle to light you to bed, you hear as you feel yourself drifting toward the coach. *Here comes a chopper to chop off your head,* as the door to the cabin shuts behind you and Clara. *Chip chop chip chop the last man is dead,* as you hear Clara's laughter outside and find yourself in the coach, alone.

They didn't even need the shock stick this time.

Since you haven't been shoved into a sack for what you suspect is your return trip to Count Drogado's mansion, you're free to look through the steamcoach's windows at the farmland outside the city.

Farms are like books on a shelf to you: interesting enough when taken individually, but at a glance they all look the same. Every barn and silo and one-story house you pass has the same dusty spine. Crooked rows of wire fence surround each square of property, and you wonder if they use steampower or chains of biodigesters for electricity. Many of your neighbors back home had a biodigester system; they were prone to explosions in hot weather, and reeked of garbage. How primitive you all were.

Alice and Beatrice keep their eyes on the back windshield, passing the bong back and forth as Beatrice mutters some kind of incantation to herself. Her lips barely move. Her third eye looks like it would burn anyone who touched it.

Alice sees you looking out the window and tells you to turn back around, punctuating her command with a belt behind your ear. Clara immediately kisses it, and you both tumble to the floor of the coach as it bounces over a thick knot in the road. You flail your arm-stump out of some residual instinct to push Clara away, and she looks at you with pity. She should.

That look puts a match to something in your heart. You roll out from under Clara and smash yourself against the door, hoping to push it open. It gives a little, but you are pulled away by Clara, who holds you in a farmgirl's grip. All four of her pupils flare wide, like little eclipses.

"We don't have time for this," Alice says. "We have to get him back to the house."

"Yes," Clara says. "We do. It won't be like before." She runs a hand up the back of your head, against the grain of your hair. "We'll protect you."

She is inviting you into the oblivion you seek, is she not? You will die in Drogado's mansion if you return, that much is certain. You will not escape again. They will load your body to the gunwales with food and liquor and vices of every kind, until there is no room left for a soul. Or they may just snap your neck on the front steps and be done with you. Think of how they "protected" Drogado's coachman.

You search for another option, but there is none. You've spent your entire life walling yourself away from options; denying yourself your parents' love and escaping to the cruelty of a city, losing your arm, then falling into indolence and becoming the kind of faceless vagrant these women would kidnap in the first place. A void opens within you whenever your mettle is tested, and you submit to it every time.

And yet, when you feel the song of death on your lips, when its whispers call to you, you reject them. You do so now, answering Clara by spitting in her pretty face.

Alice floors you with a punch that you barely feel, and you spring up towards the rear doors again. This time, they give fully, and you tumble out of the coach and down onto the road, taking the worst of the impact on your arm.

It's broken. It must be. But still, you pull yourself up and run. Where are you running? What you're running from is simple enough; the brides will pull the coach over and at least one of them—most likely Alice—will chase after you. The odds are good that she will catch you. But even if you evade her, where will you go? Back to the city, where you have nothing? Will you stake a claim in Coal Country, where the land is unfamiliar and the air strange? When the exhilaration of being chased ebbs away, and the idleness sets in, you will be lost.

And yet, something flickers within you. A will to live, however miserably, that nothing has extinguished. Is it cowardice or bravery that guides you? You grew up being taught that being brave was a matter of predestination. One either is, or is not. As you follow the curve of the road, gritting your teeth at the sudden noise of a coal truck, it occurs to you that running can be brave.

The road forks, and a narrower path leads down a hill and crosses a small creek, black with coal dust. You consider taking this path, but choose to stay on the main road. The coal truck's noise comes from everywhere at once. You don't even see it when it hits you.

Clara pushes you onto gravel. Your head is a dark mist, your body sparking all over with pain. Ribs broken again. Arm broken, too. One eye won't open.

Darkness. Then you wake up with a bitter taste in your mouth. Your eyesocket crumples in and swells up. Thick sweat crawls down your back and neck. You recognize the room you're in; it's the mirrored ballroom where you watched Count Drogado burn money. The floor is sticky with beer and trampled food.

Garbage accumulates in the room as you pass in and out of consciousness. You burrow a nest in it.

At one point you see Count Drogado, but he sounds like he is underwater. He is supervising other guests as they smash the mirrors with big hammers. Then they smash the shards into little sharp pebbles of glass that glimmer like dew.

You pass out again. You wake up and Clara is wrapping a bandage around your wrist. Blood soaks through it and rolls down your arm as slowly as sweat. Your palms and legs bear numerous cuts. Clara's second row of eyes glare at you, and behind her, Alice kicks at a pile of garbage. There is blood on her chin.

The thick scent of grease and smoke wakes you up. Beatrice is with you, her third eye exposed. Her flower garland hangs, limp and torn, from one of her ears. She presses a wet rag to your nose and mouth. She says something you can't hear. The air is heavy and hot.

You wake with a jolt and see nothing but smoke. It takes you a moment to realize that you're moving. Your arm and legs dangle over the sides of a wheelbarrow; you tilt your head back to find Alice pushing it, her face lucent with strange joy. Dust snows down from the ceiling and flames lick out from corners and open doorways. The intense heat clings to you all at once.

Drogado's house is burning.

You hear screaming all around you as other guests, their clothes in tatters, dart in and out of the smoke. Entire rooms glow yellow and orange, and fallen support beams have already burnt black. You see more flames raging through holes knocked in some of the walls, and see hammers and kerosene lanterns tossed near piles of rubble.

One voice breaks through the din for a moment. *Let us out.* The voice breaks into a cry. *Let us out of here.*

The smoke thins out enough for you to see flames crawling up support pillars and spreading across the ceiling, part of which has already caved in. The walls tear open like paper, the flames almost purple and bright enough to hurt your eyes.

Beatrice and Clara run alongside Alice as she pushes you down a hallway, then around a sharp corner, then back again when the route she'd planned is blocked by flames. Beams and studs and joists, all blackened and dead, are exposed as the foundation crumbles. More and more, this house is becoming a carcass.

Loud noises that sound like cannonfire shake the floor, which opens up under Clara. She falls too quickly to scream, and is swallowed by the flames below.

Alice screams, then shoves Beatrice away and pushes you down a hallway, toward a door that's been ripped from its hinges. She tips the wheelbarrow and sends you tumbling down one of the house's convoluted staircases.

You half-roll, half-crawl down to the bottom of the stairs, which end at a door with only enough space between them for your body. The fire hasn't touched this part of the house yet, but every surface you touch is hot.

The door bursts open and Count Drogado himself runs for the stairs, but trips over you and faceplants onto them instead. You crawl out from under him and through the door, into a carpeted hallway with fire blazing at the far end.

Moments later, a crazed-looking blond woman wearing a ruined, sand-colored gown and one elbow-length glove finds the door and kicks it fully open. As you watch, she steps on Drogado's ankle, then smashes his head against the stairs with a length of iron steampipe. When she drops the pipe and runs up the stairs, you sit there and watch Drogado twitch and bleed out in this obscure corner of his mansion. When you are certain he's breathed his last, you limp away.

You finally collapse in some fire-blackened corner and think about home, your parents' faces. You place your father in the sprawling property outside this house, watching it burn. He smiles. You smile.

Darkness.

INTERLUDE II

THE GONDOLIER

R iviere the gondolier stands in his boat, one knee bent as his foot rests on the seat. One hand clutches his long paddle in a fist, the other swings from side to side as he sings to a crowd that has gathered along the narrow sidewalks on either side of the canal. Up ahead, a small iron bridge humps over the dark water, and a crowd has gathered there, too.

Standing in a single-occupant gondola is a risky venture, especially for a man of Riviere's carriage. Flesh bulges not just at his middle, but under his arms and chin as well. The harder and louder he sings, the more it shakes, to the ascendant delight of the assembled crowd. Some of these people are tourists, but many of them work in the silt houses and scrapyards and rely on singing gondoliers like Riviere for inexpensive entertainment.

Riviere's voice fills the air as he bellows out songs in a jolly baritone. He waggles his bushy eyebrows at specific points during each song to amuse the adults. As he sings for the crowd, he scans their faces. Smiles of a certain width guarantee a coin—or better yet, a colorful bank note—tossed underhand into his boat.

He also wriggles his nose, making his bristly mustache move to amuse the children, particularly a set of three pug-nosed little girls in dirty white dresses. They watch him the way only children can, as if the rest of the world has fallen away. There are a few other children scattered throughout the audience with their parents, but these three have no obvious adult supervision at all. Nor are they smiling and clapping like the rest of the crowd. The girl on the right is pulling the middle girl's hair to the rhythm of the song, and Riviere stumbles when he sees it, but incorporates it into his routine.

Most of the other singers perform seated; Riviere is one of the few, and certainly the heaviest, who dares to stand. He rocks his gondola from side to side with his legs, teasing the possibility that he might fall into the filthy canal. The crowd buzzes with anticipation, then breaks into applause when he holds his balance. He takes a bow as coins drop into his boat.

In a corner cafe, Mrs. Grenier pours Riviere a glass of red wine, then drops an ice cube into it with her bare hand. Silver is creeping through the thin blond hair gathered into a bun behind her head.

"I don't understand why you drink it this way," she says, as she slides the glass his way. Her hand briefly touches his.

"Neither do I," Riviere says, before sipping. "But every man should have one thing about himself that he doesn't understand."

"Oh?" Mrs. Grenier perches her chin in her hand, ignoring the man to Riviere's left, who Riviere recognizes as another singing gondolier. "Is there anything else a man should have?" Aside from them and an elderly couple playing stone-a-pig at a lamp-lit rear table, the cafe is empty.

"Yes," Riviere says, after spitting the ice cube back into his glass. "A fitted shirt and some good cologne."

"Who fitted that shirt for you?" the other gondolier snorts. "A tent-maker?" He leans on his elbows and doesn't look up from the bar when he speaks.

"I borrowed this shirt from your mother," Riviere says, "so you'll have to ask her." He smiles a rosy smile and toasts the other gondolier, who responds by shoving him right off his barstool.

Lonely seaside towns are often as dirty and predictable as the water that is their livelihood. The tides rush in and draw away at their set times. The film it leaves behind—gray and silty, with a distantly foul odor—spreads across town on the soles of shoes and the sides of boxes and shipping crates. The canals form a grid of wide, central thoroughfares and narrow alleys, with numerous handmade bridges and floating docks allowing human passage. The water itself is thick and oily, and is rumored to be mostly human waste. The silt house technicians caution against swimming in it, or eating anything that comes from it, or breathing the mist that settles over it at night.

Even the trash is governed by habit; it clots in the alleys and eventually breaks off into the main canals, where the trash barges collect it.

Mrs. Grenier rolls away from Rivere's pale chest to light a cigarette.

"It's a secret," she says, "but I actually own the cafe. There's a man's name on the paperwork, but he's a ghost." She exhales smoke and scoots back toward Riviere. "Been dead for years. He was a friend of my father's."

Riviere extends an arm, making room for her as she lengthens herself against his side. "Thank god for that," he says. "If you were a man, that would make me terribly unobservant."

She laughs, nudges him with her elbow. They share a cigarette and she explains the frustrations of a woman trying to open a business on her own. On paper, her father's friend owns the cafe, and is still alive, but old and practically an invalid. On paper, she is his nurse and secretary, handling the bulk of his affairs, telling the banks and licensing clerks that he wants to open a cafe to pass down to his son when he dies.

His son is a complete fabrication. Her father's friend had two daughters, both of whom married and moved away.

Riviere listens to her and watches her arm resting on the hill his stomach makes under the sheets. He wonders if Mr. Grenier ever listens to her, enjoys the sound of her raspy voice. Her head anchors in the slope of his neck. When the cigarette is finished, Riviere flicks it out the open bedroom window and into the water. Her bedroom faces the canal, and Riviere tenses every time a boat passes by.

"Why open a cafe at all," he asks, "when it is such a hassle?" "So that I can sell it," she says, "and travel. Maybe go Overseas before I get too old to move around."

Riviere nods. "How does your husband feel about this?"

She rolls out of bed. Her body is tan and lean, and he pulls the sheets around him to cover his pale, flabby chest and limbs. She walks to the window, making no attempt to cover her nudity until she pulls the curtains shut.

Riviere's basement apartment is small, dark, and split into two rooms; one is his bedroom and the other is a small dining room with an icebox and an electric steamplate that sparks if it's left on too long. His bed is a thin mattress on the bare concrete floor. He does not live the way a man should live, is what his father and uncles would say if they saw his situation.

His gondola is tethered in the alley behind his apartment, in a tapered strip of water that he keeps as free of garbage as possible. He sleeps in it more than he does his apartment, and has considered forsaking the apartment altogether. There are nights where he could swear that the walls were being cinched in around him, and the ceiling lowered.

Sometimes Riviere takes his gondola out at night to wander the canals. The water could pass for pretty when it reflects the lamps, and Riviere has grown to appreciate stretches of time where he isn't vying for attention.

He paddles up and down the central canals, using his hands to help the boat navigate corners. On one particularly long stretch of water, he lies on his back and stares up at the sky as his boat drifts with the current. Most of the time, the sky is a solid sheet of black, the stars no larger than pinpricks.

Alone and adrift, Riviere's mind wanders. Beyond the buzzing of the lamps, the distant sounds of clockwork weirs adjusting the canals' water levels and controlling their flow, and the occasional bird call or human voice, the town is dark and still. Riviere's boat drifts through long patches of stillness, the kind of dense quiet that almost mimics sound, the kind that makes Riviere nervous and raises goosebumps on his arms and legs.

Riviere lets a hand dangle in the water, forgetting that it is polluted. A balled up a scrap of paper bumps against his hand, and he pulls it up from the water. It's the kind of paper that butchers wrap meat in, and he holds it up to the lamplight as he passes under it. Afterward, he throws it into the air. It unfurls into a bird and flies away.

That night, Riviere dreams of those three little girls walking across a gray desert for miles. The dunes follow the familiar slopes and valleys of Riviere's body, and sand shifts and sprays with the wind as he tries to cover himself. An old woman leans a white bicycle against a cactus and follows them into a crowd of desiccated pilgrims beating their fists into the ground as sand rips the flesh from their faces, calling out for the sun, the sun, the sun.

A saltfish man paddles his snub-nosed boat through the canals, calling out his wares in a voice that skips across the water. When someone obliges, they throw money into his boat and he extends a thick white strip of salted fish to them on the end of a pointed stick. Customers mostly pull it off with their hands, but a few use their teeth, which the saltfish man regards as barbaric.

His boat passes Riviere's gondola, and they greet each other as salesmen and performers do, with genial suspicion. The saltfish man asks if Riviere would like one on the house, and the singer obliges. The stick is not necessary for this transaction.

"Delicious," Riviere says, licking his fingers. "What kind of fish is this?"

"Do you write your own songs?" replies the saltfish man, and they both laugh at questions they are too professional to answer.

As Riviere wipes sweat back through his hair, he points at the saltfish man's stick. "You should use tongs to pass that fish around. That thing will scare people."

"Tongs cut the meat," the saltfish man says. He is small, with curly auburn hair and a beard to match, and he drums his thin fingers on the lid of his saltfish box as he talks. "They're too hard to control at the length I'd need." He hefts the stick so Riviere can see its full construction. "This is perfect though, and look, it's weighted at my end."

"For what purpose?" Riviere asks.

"So I can pull people into the canal if they try to cross me." Some of the humor drains from the saltfish man's voice. Riviere nods, and is about to comment on the day's heat when he catches his reflection in the water.

"Are you all right?" the saltfish man says, squinting as the sun hits his eyes. Riviere coughs and spits into the water.

"Yes, why?"

"Looked like you saw something down there."

"I did," Riviere says. "Something unpleasant. It's gone now." He leaves it at that.

The midday sun pulls sweat from Riviere's body as he paddles down the canal, singing to a small but responsive group on the sidewalk that follows him like a team of ducklings.

When the bow of Riviere's boat nudges a collapsed building, he steps onto the ruins, holding his gondola in place with his paddle as he sings to them. On the spot, he launches into one of his parents' favorite songs about a building that collapses because the newlyweds on the top floor enjoy each others' company so vigorously. The song is sung from the point of view of their elderly landlady, whose agitation hides a certain amount of envy.

Riviere is halfway into the bawdiest verse when he sees those three girls again, staring at him from the crowd. He stutters a little, only having a split second to decide whether or not to continue the song, but soldiers on. He even waves at them, and they wave back. One of them has a red, sticky-looking hand.

Gripping each brick with his toes, Riviere walks along the spine of the collapsed building. They are not uncommon in town; over time, the water laps away

at the foundations of houses and other structures
and leaves gritty salt deposits on the windows. Many
buildings in town show cow patches of new bricks and
mortar where their occupants have repaired them. This
building, whatever it was, has fallen across the alley
and made itself a stage for Riviere.

When his song is finished, the crowd tosses coins into
his gondola. One of the little girls is smiling as her
sister tosses something that lands with a thud near the
gondola's stern.

Later, Riviere finds a dead bird in his boat.

Unlike other singing gondoliers, Riviere doesn't perform
in the central marketplace if he can help it. He only goes
when he needs to buy food for the week, always making
sure to move between thickets of other shoppers as they
pick out fresh poultry and fish, and examine produce in
long troughs full of ice. The stands and stalls are set up
on parallel docks, with square floating platforms tethered
together on the water for the public. It's one of the only
parts of town cut off from boat and gondola travel.

Riviere steps cautiously, keeping his wide-brimmed hat
pulled low to shade his face, filling his wicker basket
with groceries. As lucrative as his weight can be for his

performances, it is a disadvantage here, and every step he takes is accompanied by the fear that it will sink or upend one of the floating platforms and send unsuspecting shoppers flailing into the dirty canal water. It also marks him as Riviere, outgoing singer, when all he wants is to be Riviere, citizen, and left alone.

He sees Mrs. Grenier at a fruit-seller's stand, examining the produce as a line forms behind her. A man with dark, wavy hair and a prominent nose stands with her, holds her hand. It's not a big nose. Just a prominent one. He has the heavy, stooped shoulders of someone who works in the silt houses.

They are picking through a pyramid stack of apples, holding each one and squeezing. The seller is babbling recipe ideas at them, trying to engage them into buying something, but they ignore him, except to say "this one's too soft" or "this one looks sour." Every time an apple fails inspection, they put it on top of the stack, and a few of them roll off into the water. Riviere watches them as other people shove and jostle past him on the crowded platforms.

The seller, anxious to get them away before they drive off more business, pulls an ice crate from behind his stall and pries it open. "Champagne mangoes," he says. "Imported. Sweet with a buttery texture."

Mr. Grenier holds one. "How do you eat it?"

"Peel it with a cheese knife and eat it out of your hand." The seller's tone makes it clear that he wants to be telling them something else, like where to go and how to get there.

The Greniers buy two and stroll away, and Riviere stands there and watches them, even as the protective buffer of other people around him thins away. Mrs. Grenier turns around and he looks away, not sure where to focus. There are suddenly too many mouths and voices, too many eyes leaving blemishes on him. His stomach screws into itself, begging him to retreat to someplace quiet and empty.

As he walks back to his gondola, he thinks about them sharing a mango as their bedsheets air-dry, then dressing the bed before making love on it. He tries to push those images from his mind. He cannot. Instead, he paddles home to put his groceries away in his tiny icebox and smoke a cigarette.

A white bicycle leans against a weathered brick house cornering an alley. Had it not caught the edge of the lamp light, Riviere wouldn't have seen it at all. Bicycles were uncommon, and useless, in a town on the water, so he wasn't in the habit of seeing them. The only reason he recognizes it at all is because he grew up on land.

A candle is still burning inside this corner house, and Riviere holds his boat still, examining the scene. He isn't expecting to find anything, but merely obeys the whim of some low-humming curiosity. The house is four stories and wider than average, and some of the masonry near the water has been repaired. A trash barrel sits by the front steps. Besides the candle, there is no other light within the house.

Riviere waits there for a half hour, letting his attention slowly wander until the front door opens. An old woman, dressed smartly in city clothes, with one fist clenched. A chord is struck in Riviere's mind; he has seen this woman before. But where? This is beyond simple recognition, she seems familiar to him. He paddles across the canal to her as she unlocks the chain securing her bicycle.

"Evening, madam," Riviere says, smiling at her. She turns to him with a look he reads as either disbelief or surprise.

"Good evening," she says.

"Lovely night, wouldn't you agree?" Riviere smooths his mustache with his fingers. "Say, do I know you from somewhere?"

"I wouldn't know," the old lady says, mounting the bicycle.

"No? Are you a visitor, then?" Riviere is puzzled, but still smiles. "Strange, I could have sworn. Well, if you're still here tomorrow, come back and I'll sing for you."

The old lady turns, still seated on the bicycle, and her eyes harden. "Hopefully you won't see me at all the next time I'm here." She pedals away and Riviere lets himself float in the opposite direction. He feels dejected for a moment, and then kicks himself for not asking her more about her bicycle.

The following day, he paddles back to that house and sees funeral shrouds across the door. Several people stand outside, their heads bowed. He hears the tone of deep red bells sounding from upstream, signaling the black pontoon that will float the deceased to the man-made lake designated as the town cemetery. After the religious service, the funereal anchor will be attached, and the deceased will be sent overboard.

Riviere quickly reroutes, deciding to sing elsewhere.

Riviere bathes three times a week in the common washroom above his basement apartment. He prefers bathing at night, even though the hot water is limited by then, because there are fewer interruptions from other tenants. Not to mention, bathing and then immediately going out into town and getting dirty is a waste.

When Riviere bathes, it is with his eyes shut, standing in the stone stall under a brass shower nozzle. He will not open his eyes until he has thrown a shirt over his body, and bathes with the door and window shut to fog up the mirror near the sink.

Fat idiot, he mutters to himself as his steam-pressed soap turns to lather in his hands. *Whatever devil's bargain you struck to bed Mrs. Grenier, don't think it won't come back to find you.* He thinks of her and wonders how she is not insulted by the sight of him expanding in her bed like a pool of water.

The three little girls appear outside the cafe as Riviere paddles up to it and ties his gondola to a cleat. They make a triangle on the narrow sidewalk, all facing one another, shuffling their little hands behind their backs. Riviere watches them for a moment before climbing up onto the sidewalk. The exertion makes him grunt, and breaks the girls' concentration. They open their eyes in unison and turn toward him. One of them is smiling.

"I'm Clara," she says, "and this is Beatrice, and Alice." She gestures to the other two, who glare at her.

"Shhhh," Alice says, pressing her finger to her lips. "Don't talk to strangers."

Riviere smiles. "Wise counsel, but I'm not a stranger. You saw me singing yesterday." He introduces himself. The girls' faces soften, but not much. "What are you playing?" Riviere asks.

"We're playing pass the slipper," Clara says, wiping her hands on her white dress. Her eyes are large and bright, and entirely black, and she wears her hair low on her forehead, unlike the other two. "Do you want to play?"

"I'm not sure I know how," Riviere says. He is interrupted by a stream of people running past as another gondola singer—dark hair, leathery skin, tattoos on both forearms—paddles upstream. He and the girls press their backs against the cafe's brick facade until the singer leads his audience away.

"So how do you play?" he asks Clara.

"Don't tell him," Alice says. "He won't do it right."

"Two of us sing and pass the slipper behind our backs, and the third has to guess which one has it when we stop," Clara says, beaming up at Riviere until Alice punches her in the arm.

"You should push her in the canal," Beatrice says to Alice.

"Girls, please!" Riviere steps away from them. The last thing he wants to be associated with is children fighting. His reputation would suffer. "There's no need to argue. I tell you what, the three of you can play and I'll just sing."

He watches them mull it over. "It's up to you."

Alice nods, but also pouts. "Fine," she says. "One game." She moves next to Beatrice, and Clara stands in front of them. She closes her eyes when Riviere starts to sing; he picks a short nursery rhyme, not knowing how long the song was supposed to be. When he stops, Clara opens her eyes, studies the other two girls for a moment, then points to Beatrice. Beatrice produces the slipper from behind her back and throws it to the ground in disgust.

"It's not fair," she says. "He didn't sing long enough." Clara protests this, and in an instant they're bickering and shoving each other again. Riviere tries to calm things down and gets his foot stomped on for his troubles.

The noise attracts some attention, mostly stares and pointing from people who don't engage otherwise, and an older woman in working clothes comes out of the cafe, jabbing her cane at the girls.

"Go on! Get! Get out of here!" she growls as the girls run away. Riviere leans against the cafe's facade again, putting his weight on his unstomped foot.

"Don't pay those girls any mind," the old woman tells him. She is round, like he is, and short, but there is a great urgency in her voice and movements, as if she were a heavy spring on the verge of harmonic motion. "They're nothing but trouble. Wild, all three of 'em."

"Someone should talk with their parents, then," Riviere said.

"Never seen 'em. My guess is debtor's prison. They wouldn't be the only unclaimed children in town." The old woman spits into the canal. "Just the worst of 'em." She shuffles back into the cafe, and this time, Riviere follows her. Mrs. Grenier greets him with a glass of chilled red wine, and they leave for her house as soon as he's finished.

This time, it is Riviere who rolls away from Mrs. Grenier, folding into himself once he is safely on his side. He had been running his hand along the flatness of her stomach until pangs of self-consciousness about his own stayed his hand. He felt her hand trailing up and down his back.

"Are you all right?" she asks.

"Your husband is real, yes?" Riviere stares at the window, but not through it. His eyes trace the muntin bars over and over. "Yes," Mrs. Grenier says. "He is. Of course he is."

"Real like the man's name on your paperwork, or actually real?"

"What is this?" she asks, annoyed. "You're sulking."

"I've never met him," Riviere says, "or heard his name outside this bedroom. It's just odd, is all."

"My husband doesn't make friends easily," Mrs. Grenier says. "Or at all, really. It's stifling. He works at the silt house and drinks alone in the kitchen. That is his life."

"Then why marry him?"

Mrs. Grenier sighs, turning over onto her back and pulling the sheets up over her breasts. "Because I had to marry someone."

"No you didn't—"

"To have options? Yes, I did." Mrs. Grenier pulls some of the sheets away from him. "Having men's names attached to mine, even if they are lies, has gotten me a lot farther than honesty would have."

"That makes me sad," is all Riviere can say.

"It should."
Four boats pass by the window before Riviere speaks again. "I'm sorry about the sheets."

"What?"

"I've messed them up. They must take forever to clean after I've been here." He bows his head.

"Riviere, there's nothing wrong with the sheets. What has gotten into you?"

Riviere tongue darts across his teeth. "Are you attracted to me?"

"You're being a child," is her response. More silence follows, during which Mrs. Grenier dozes off. Riviere listens to her snore as he turns and compares her body to his. The way the sheets bulge around him, his body looks like two uneven scoops of sherbet. He feels like sherbet, a palate cleanser between what Mrs. Grenier has already been served, and what she really wants.

He gets dressed without waking her and leaves through the door at the back of the kitchen.

Riviere sings twice that evening, picking melancholy songs about unrequited love both times; if he must cry, he might as well do it for money. Among the volley of coins tossed into his boat is the limp body of a seagull, its neck broken. He lifts it up to throw it back on the sidewalk and sees the three little girls, the orphans, staring down at him.

"Did you do this?" he asks.

"You already ruined one game for us," Alice says. "Don't ruin another one." Blood is smeared down the front of her white dress.

He waits until they leave to drop the bird in the water.

Riviere is stirred from sleep by an ashy smell, and finds himself fully dressed in his gondola, floating through an unfamiliar neighborhood. The houses are smaller, drawn in tighter against one another, unlit. Riviere's gondola passes more than one gloomy doorway with someone sleeping in it, their head resting against the jamb and their body crooked on the steps. Voices both unseen and unfriendly waft through the darkness.

Those are the only details Riviere observes before he concentrates fully on leaving the area. He doesn't see the garland of flowers hanging from the iron railing on the house's front steps, or the dead pigeons and rats littering the sidewalk.

The next day, Riviere sings only once. He tethers his boat at the cathedral, knotting his tie-line in the mouth of one of the fearsome saltstone lions at the base of the steps. The evening breeze carries garbage smells that dry out his throat and sting his eyes. His mighty voice cracks a few times and his brain burns in his head with shame. To compensate, he pours on the theatrics, jiggling the loose skin under his chin and arms to make the crowd laugh.

This crowd is looser, more reactive than most, probably because they are younger. A lot of the older townspeople, the ones who've been toiling in the silt house and scrapyards for years, are often too tired to do much besides passively enjoy a song or two before dinner. The young, though, want to carouse, and they bring that energy with them everywhere, even to singers on the canal. They cheer, whistle, and throw money without prompt as they dance on the sidewalks and steps.

Most of the men are dressed casually, in billowing shirts and trousers that allow airflow, and the women wear simple dresses that leave their arms and collarbones bare. Riviere clutches his own body as he sings, adjusting his trousers and blousing out his shirt in response to their bodies, figuring shapelessness is better than his natural shape. More than once he considers stopping and paddling home.

The three girls—Alice, Beatrice, and Clara—appear at the front of the crowd. Beatrice has a bruise around her eye, and Alice has a swollen lip. They are all smiles, smeared head to toe with dirt. Riviere shakes his head as Clara tosses something at his boat; it banks off the side and into the canal.

Alice and Beatrice turn on Clara, and before anyone can intervene, they beat on her with their little fists. The crowd hollows out around them, and someone runs off to find a policeman, while others try and pull the girls apart.

"Give the coin back!" Alice keeps shouting, even as her partnership with Beatrice dissolves and the three girls swing on each other without discrimination.

Riviere's stomach buckles and he dives into the canal without thinking. His eyes are clenched tight against the water as he smacks his way to the greasy bottom of the canal. He only has a few moments to find a coin and hope they accept it. His lungs already hurt. His hands scramble over sunken things, half-eaten away by the water.

He stirs a coin up from the grime and makes a fist around it, then pushes himself up to the surface again. Taking big, greedy gulps of air, he drops the coin—coated with river sludge and impossible to identify—on the sidewalk. Most of the crowd has dispersed, and a policeman has helped three other onlookers separate the girls. He releases Clara so she can pick up the coin.

As she leans down, her hair falls loose, exposing two more eyes in her forehead. Riviere's eyes dart away from that, and he sees Beatrice winding the flower garland, now torn and bloody, back around her head. Riviere only catches a glimpse of a third eye, red enough to mimic the setting sun, as the garland covers it.

The policeman loads the girls into his patrol boat and takes them away, while Riviere climbs back into his gondola to count his money. The puddle he leaves around the seat is black.

A tall, thin man approaches Riviere on the street.

"Do you have a cigarette, perchance?" the man asks.

Riviere tries to smile, but cannot. His eyes are dark pits in his doughy face. He is watching the police pull a small white dress from the canal and attempt to flap it dry. "Who do you suppose that belonged to?" he asks the stranger.

"I'm not sure," the man says. He tilts his chin, perplexed, and absently kicks a chunk of masonry into the water. Riviere leaves without saying another word, and drops a crumpled parcel of cigarettes at the man's feet as he walks away. There are two cigarettes left in it.

The gondola's water-worn appearance is made plain. The paint is cracking and peeling, salt deposits are visible above the waterline, and the structure is bowing out, as if being crushed flat by the weight of its main occupant.

Riviere paddles past Mrs. Grenier's cafe, his hat drawn low over his face, and he docks in a neighborhood he rarely visits. He walks into the first public house whose door is open, sits down at the bar, and calls for red wine.

"I used to drink this stuff cold," he says to the barkeep. "Can you imagine? I don't do that anymore." The barkeep snorts a response and goes back to rinsing out pint glasses.

After one glass of wine, Riviere returns to his gondola. He sees people milling around up ahead, and small boats for hire ferrying people down the canal. He takes a deep breath and paddles toward them, hoping the red wine will enrich his voice. He must sing. There is nothing else to do.

He thinks, briefly, that he sees a white bicycle leaning against a lamp post, but decides that he does not.

EPILOGUE

The old woman carries the bag into the farmhouse and, with great deliberation, empties it onto the floor. She reassembles it as best she can, being careful not to dislodge the man's coin when she twists his skull back onto his spine.

She cannot heal his cracked ribs or fractured arm, or his crushed orbital bones. All she can do is remove her spectacles and stare into his eyesockets until the bones tremble against the floor.

"Write for me," she says, then pulls the skeleton up and guides it down a hallway and through a door, into a barren room with a desk and chair. A thick stack of paper appears in her right hand, and she sets it down, along with a pen.

"I don't know what to say," the skeleton says.

"Tell me how you got here," the old woman says as she walks out and shuts the door behind her.

The old woman paces outside the door. Her shoes clack against the floor. She turns to the left and clicks her tongue, then turns back to the right. A simple wooden chair appears next to her.

The old woman smiles and sits down. Five minutes pass before a sheet of long paper slips out from under the door. She picks it up and examines the tight, scrawled handwriting.

You woke up here. It is dark. You are naked.

She frowns at his opening sentences, then takes the paper into her coin room and finds an empty ledger for it.

More pages come, and the old woman learns his name: Thomas Carey.

The pages pile up under the door, and get added to their assigned ledger one by one. One sheet has a thin strip has been torn from the
bottom, which unsettles the old woman until that missing strip slides out into the hallway. *Can I have a blanket?* it says. *I'm cold in here.*

The old woman sighs and closes her eyes. She clears her throat, then opens her eyes again. A light blue cotton blanket is draped over her chair. She pulls it onto the floor and feeds it under the door with her foot.

While he writes, she continues collecting and filing coins. His presence in the house and the writing that greets her when she returns home have unexpected side effects. She finds herself riding her bicycle when she doesn't have to, welcoming the ache in her legs, the wind in her face, the transitions between smooth pavement, rough brick, round cobblestones. Friction becoming momentum.

One of the coins she files away belongs to Count Drogado, of whom she has gotten a full portrait from

Mr. Carey's writings. His coin has been worn smooth and black, with misshapen edges. He was an idiot, it would seem. A simple creature of lust who'd gotten in way over his head. *Death is a gift,* the old woman thinks as she puts his coin away. *I am a gift to you.*

Two of the brides' coin sleeves remain empty. The old woman grunts as she pushes a brittle, broken penny into Clara's designated sleeve.

When the last sheet of paper slides out into the hallway, the old woman reads it with a heavy heart. *Darkness* is the final word.

Thomas Carey's skeleton drops the pen on the desk and stands up to crack his knees and back. It is then that he realizes his condition and almost undoes the old woman's handiwork by falling to pieces. He looks at his hand, then the rest of his bones, and sits back down in a panic. Under normal circumstances, his breath would quicken, but he has no lungs. He raps his knuckles against the desk until the sharp sound disturbs him enough to make him stop.

He slides his last sheet of paper under the door and waits. Sitting down again, he crosses one leg over the other, rapping the desk again as his bones touch. He runs his hand over the fractures in his ribs and feels a piece break away, hears it hit the ground.

"Don't do that," the old woman says as she reenters the room. "I'm not assembling you twice." She picks up the piece of rib and puts it on the desk. "Are you finished?"

"I don't have anything left to say," Thomas tells her.

"I know," she says. "You've said plenty. More than I expected."

"What did you want to know?" he asks.
"A lot," she says, "and most of it is above your head, Mr. Carey." She glances upward for a moment, then locks eyes with him again. "But whatever mystery you posed to me has been solved, so that's good, at least."

He isn't sure how to take that, and tells her so.

"What I mean," she says, "is that the interplay between your melancholy and survival instincts is fascinating. The very thing that made you desire death so plainly, enough that you could see me, made you deny it at every turn."

He nods. There it is, then. His life, in two sentences.

"It's like you want something that you know you'll never get," he says, "but you know you'll never stop wanting it, either."

"Yes," the old woman says, "exactly that. And now, I think we've reached the end." She approaches him and reaches for his ear.

"Wait," he says. She does.

"Is this it?" he asks. "Is this all there is?"

"Sometimes, yes," she says. "What else did you want?"

"I wanted to know who I really am," he says. "I was so... whatever I was, I was that, all the time."

"Melancholy."

"More than that," he says. "Sad, listless, angry, all of those things, and whatever they mix together to be. I never got the chance to find out if I could be anything else."

"Not everyone does," the old woman says. Before Thomas Carey can answer that, she grabs the spot where his ear would have been.

The old woman holds Thomas Carey's coin up to the light. A nickel-plated five cent piece with a keelboat reverse. Significant environmental damage and discoloration, but the embossed image is still present. It has endured better than the coins of richer and ultimately more benevolent people.

Leaving his body where it is—it's not going anywhere, after all—the old woman walks out of the room, and the house, past the washwomen scrubbing through a mountain of blood-spattered laundry. The coin will be cleaned and reassigned. It is the least she can do.

No. The least she could do would be nothing. She will take one step further.

Rest, now. You are dead.

DAVE K.

Dave K's work has been published in Front Porch Journal, Battered Suitcase, Cobalt, Queen Mob's Tea House, Welter, Truck, and The Avenue, among others. He is also the author of *stone a pig* (2012) and *MY NAME IS HATE* (2014). He is also also a marine gastropod mollusk in the family Conidae.

The author would like to thank his friends and family for their support, specifically Evangeline Ridgaway, Melissa LaMartina, Beth Brown, the Baltimore Rock Opera Society, Abby Higgs, Justin Sanders, and the members of his writing group in Baltimore. The author would also like to acknowledge the music to which this book was written: Neko Case, Weyes Blood, Torrid Husk, Blood Mist, Verbum Mentis, Windhand, Batushka, Wing Dam, and Natural Velvet.

MORE FROM
MASON JAR PRESS

Not Without Our Laughter | Poetry
by The Black Ladies Brunch Collective

A collection of humorous and joyful poems–riffing on Langston Hughes's Not Without Laughter–that explores topics of family, work, and sexuality.

Notes From My Phone* | Memoir
by Michelle Junot

Michelle Junot has kept notes on her phone for years, all while creating a snapshot of her life with an honesty that only occurs when not paying attention. In Notes From My Phone*, Junot opens up her phone and her life to you.

Caligula's Playhouse | Poetry
by Stephen Zerance

Blasphemous. Pagan. Sex and satyrs and pop culture dominate this dark, funny collection of poems dealing with the body. Love it. Fear it.

Learn more at masonjarpress.xyz.